PRISONERS OF THE NVA

"Come on, Colonel! You're the leader . . . are you going to let your soldier die?" Van Pao demanded.

Colonel Garibaldi's lower lip trembled. He was ashamed, but he didn't have the courage to take Spencer Barnett's place.

Spencer saw what the female NVA lieutenant was doing—she was going to kill him, but at the same time she was going to totally break the colonel.

"Hey! Sweet Bitch! I won't let him take my place!" Barnett screamed. "Damn you, sir! Don't you fall for this shit! You know the game she's playing!"

One of the guards kicked Spencer in the side to shut him up and he yelled all the louder.

"Colonel! You've got to live for both of us!"

Lieutenant Van Pao barked orders to the guards, and they picked Spencer up and placed him directly over the sharpened bamboo stake . . .

P.O.W.
SURVIVOR OF NAM '2

Also by Donald E. Zlotnik

Survivor of Nam: Baptism
Survivor of Nam: Black Market*
Survivor of Nam: Court-Martial*

Published by
POPULAR LIBRARY

*forthcoming

P.O.W.
SURVIVOR OF NAM #2

DONALD E. ZLOTNIK

POPULAR LIBRARY

An Imprint of Warner Books, Inc.

A Warner Communications Company

Dear Mom and Dad,

Things have been quiet for a while and I've actually gotten some time to catch up on my letter writing—not that there is anything really new. In fact, after a while being a soldier is just like any other job, except maybe that you carry a gun... and you don't get to go home at five o'clock.

Reggie said to say thanks for the clothes for the kids. He's almost finished making arrangements to send them home to his folks. Both of them are so cute, you almost would believe that they didn't know there was a war going on, but they do. Kids are kids.

Love,

David

CHAPTER ONE

A Rum

She flicked out her tongue and instantly sensed the change of temperature between the air and the warm rock she was lying on and moved her coils so that the bottom of her long body could enjoy the heat coming from the sun-warmed surface. A flash of light from the side of the mountain on the opposite side of the river registered in her slow-to-function brain as something different, but not threatening to her safety. It had been ten years since anything had even tried bothering her. There was no way for her to know that she was the largest living reticulated python in the world. She was a little over thirty-six feet long and had a girth of thirty-nine inches.

Lieutenant Van Pao held her field glasses up to her eyes and watched the iridescent skin of the large python flash in a beautiful rainbow of colors. The snake had just come out of the water and contrasted with the sand-colored flat rock she had crawled on. Lieutenant Van Pao looked at her watch; this was the fifth morning in a row that the python had come out of the river onto the rock. The North Vietnamese lieutenant was sure that it had a burrow near the basking place and used the sun-heated rock to raise her body temperature before going hunting along the fast-flowing mountain river.

* * *

The area around the prison compound had been cleared of underbrush, and a twenty-foot circle of pungi stakes separated the camp from the Bru Montagnard village of A Rum in Laos. The pungi stakes weren't very effective as a fence, but they issued a clear warning to the villagers and to the prisoners of war that any attempt to cross the open ground would result in their being shot by one of the NVA guards.

Corporal Barnett carried the bundles of freshly cut bamboo poles over each one of his shoulders. He dropped the load off his right shoulder first and then leaned to his left side so that the bundle could roll off his collarbone to the ground.

"What do you think they're building?"

The Air Force colonel looked up from tying two of the poles together with a long piece of split bamboo. "You've got me, Spencer. It could be another POW cage. . . ."

"Naw, I don't think so, they're building it too low for that."

"Maybe it's for *short* Vietnamese?" The colonel joked but Barnett was concentrating too hard on the purpose of the new cage to catch the pun.

"They've always kept the South Vietnamese prisoners separate from us Americans."

"Well then, the only thing we can do is wait and see!" The colonel reached over for another one of the long poles Barnett had just delivered and spaced it with the others that had already been tied to the frame of the cage. "It is a little unusual to have the bamboo spaced so close together, and putting the gate on *top* of the cage doesn't make any sense at all."

A guard noticed Barnett and the colonel talking and yelled over to the prisoners to get back to work.

Barnett went back to the edge of the camp, where an NVA soldier was using a machete to cut and trim the bamboo poles. The NVA soldier was sweating and angry; he had been detailed for the hard labor because he had been caught sleeping on guard the night before. Barnett felt the flat side of the wide knife-blade against his shoulder and jerked away instinctively. The guard curled his upper lip and pointed to the pile of bamboo. Barnett looked down at the ground and then went over to assemble another load. The week before, he would have glared at the young NVA guard and been beaten for his insolence. The Air Force colonel was teaching him how to survive in the NVA prisoner-of-war compound, but it was against everything Barnett believed in to subjugate himself to other humans, especially the young guard who had just hit him with the machete.

The sound of soft laughter floated across the narrow clearing to where Barnett was working with the bamboo. He snuck a look out of the corner of his eye and saw Mohammed James sitting on the shaded porch of the Montagnard house. The sound of laughter increased when James saw Barnett sneak a look in his direction. He pulled the fifteen-year-old Montagnard girl closer to him and put her hand on his crotch. She giggled when she felt the bulge, and he laughed louder.

"*Hey! Barnett!* Do you want to fuck my woman?" James yelled across the pungi-staked barrier. He had been drinking *num-pah,* a rice wine fermented in large, ten-gallon earthenware crocks and drunk directly from the crock with a bamboo straw.

Barnett ignored James's comment, picked up another load of bamboo poles, and started walking back toward the new cage.

"*Hey, you motherfucker!*" James stood up and screamed at Barnett, who had turned his back to him. "*Who the fuck do you think you are! Huh?*"

Barnett continued walking away.

"I'm going to smoke your white ass! *Do you hear me?*" James heard the girl giggle and grabbed her by the arm. "*You* respect *me! You hear?*" He staggered into the dark longhouse the NVA had forced the Montagnards to build for him and pulled the girl behind him.

The Air Force colonel had heard James screaming over at

Barnett and was smiling when the young soldier returned with his load. "That was smart, Spencer."

Barnett dropped his load and glared over at the colonel. "I'm going to kill that motherfucking traitor before I leave here!"

"He'll get his; you just stay calm and *survive*."

"It's hard . . ." said Barnett, whispering under his breath.

"I know . . . I know, Spencer, but you've got to tune him out." The colonel fitted a piece of bamboo against the frame. "They're looking for any excuse to make an example out of you . . . *anything!* There's something they want from you, or they would have executed you the first time you tried to punch out a guard." The colonel lowered his voice, speaking without moving his lips. "Do you know what they're after?"

Barnett kept busy stacking the poles near the colonel. "I guess it has to do with the seismic-intrusion detectors my recon team had planted right before we were ambushed."

"But you said that James's team had planted six of them also . . . it doesn't make sense." The colonel stopped talking when the roving guard neared their workplace, waiting until the NVA soldier wandered on before continuing. "There has to be something else."

Barnett shrugged his shoulders. "Every time Sweet Bitch calls me in for interrogation, she asks about the green boxes we planted and where they're located. . . . 'I've told you everything that I know about those boxes, Colonel Garibaldi. . . .'"

"I believe you, Spencer. . . . When I was working in the Pentagon, there were rumors that we had special seismic devices that could be air dropped. They were about two feet long and had antennae that looked like young saplings . . . that could easily have been changed to bamboo." The colonel frowned, trying to recall something else from the top-secret briefing. There was something else about the detectors that he knew was very important, but he couldn't remember what it was.

Barnett left and went back for another load of bamboo. The colonel spent the rest of the afternoon trying to recall every detail from the briefing that had taken place years earlier.

Lieutenant Van Pao returned to her office in the village right before noon. She was well pleased with the results of her engineers. The village of A Rum looked exactly like it had before they moved the POW camp and her headquarters into it. A great deal of care had been taken to blend the new longhouses and storage areas with the existing village. Aerial photographs would reveal only a slightly larger village, something that was common in the war-torn countryside where the Montagnards had gathered together for protection against bombings. The Americans refused to bomb the settlements as long as they remained Montagnard and there was no sign of NVA activity near them.

The field telephone in her small office emitted a loud buzzing sound that startled her. She reached for the black handset and answered the direct line to division headquarters.

"Lieutenant Van Pao speaking, sir!"

There was a short pause filled with static, and then a deep voice spoke. "Lieutenant, when are we going to get some information on those sensors the Americans have placed along the Ho Chi Minh Trail?"

"Sir! I have been working on the American soldier, but he has been very stubborn during interrogations."

"You mean to tell me that you cannot break one seventeen-year-old soldier?" The senior officer's voice was filled with contempt. "Should I send a *professional* officer to your camp to *help?*"

"No sir! I am sure that I can break the soldier and get the information we need!"

"If the devices our friend Mohammed James showed us had been removed *professionally,* we wouldn't still be waiting!" The old intelligence officer was angry with the woman because she had allowed the six seismic-intrusion detectors to be moved that the American named James had shown them before checking to see if they had been booby-trapped.

All of the devices had special tilt mechanisms in them, so that once they had been implanted and turned on, they couldn't be moved without a small explosive charge destroying the insides of the green boxes. "I want the other six sensors found before the end of this week! Do you understand me, Lieutenant?"

"Yes sir!"

"We have already lost over five hundred replacements because of those sensors, as well as sixty trucks that cannot be replaced!" The officer's voice was rising in anger. "If James didn't know about the destruction devices, I am sure this other American doesn't know about them either!"

"Sir . . . he won't talk about anything! He won't even confirm his *name*!"

"Get him to talk! Or you'll be back in the field as an intelligence officer at Cu Chi!" The telephone went dead.

She placed the receiver back in its cradle and went over to the open window that was covered with shutters to blot out the light at night and to keep out the rain during the monsoons. She knew that she had to do something fast about Spencer Barnett, for two reasons: her honor, and because she knew that she couldn't survive living underground in the tunnels at Cu Chi. There you could live for six months underground without ever coming to the surface. She hated tunnels, and the intelligence officer at division knew that about her.

"Sergeant!" She screamed the word through the open window. A small, chubby man in his late fifties popped into her office. He was a well-decorated NCO and had fought in some of the great battles for independence, including Dien Bien Phu. The years, plus being wounded eight times, had forced him to serve in a noncombatant role, and he was very unhappy.

"Yes, Lieutenant?"

"I want a detail platoon ready to depart tomorrow at dawn." She turned her back on the sergeant. "Have them bring the fish nets and the large rice bags from my office."

"Do you want them to forage again this week?" The sergeant was slightly puzzled, because they had just foraged from two smaller Montagnard villages up the valley, and there was plenty of fresh meat in the village for the camp cadre.

"No . . . we are going hunting for *wild* game." She smiled and added an afterthought. "Make sure Dong Bec is a member of the detail. He was a professional trapper back home, wasn't he?"

"Yes, Lieutenant. He says that he's even trapped tigers." The sergeant's eyebrows rose slightly.

"Good! Make sure they are ready!" She left her office and strolled over to the hooch where the American lived with his Montagnard girlfriend.

The water was cold, but not as cold as her burrow. She took her time entering the water and swam just under the surface with only her head above water. A view from directly overhead made her look as if she were floating in the air.

The river water was crystal clear. A large garfish darted out of her way and hid under a rock overhang until she had passed. The river narrowed between two flat boulders and formed a short rapids that forced her to take to the land for a short crawl of less than a hundred meters before the river widened again and formed a series of large, deep pools. There her favorite basking place was on the surface of a house-sized flat rock, which was positioned near the edge of the river where it caught the earliest rays of the morning sun. She approached her rock from the river and took her time bringing all of her thirty-six feet of coils up on the dry stone.

Lieutenant Van Pao smiled. She was on time as usual. A shiver rippled down the NVA lieutenant's spine. The python was even larger close up than she had anticipated. One of the soldiers in hiding stifled a scream and tried backing up to get away from the huge reptile. None of the NVA platoon had been told *what* they were going to capture and take back to the camp. The python was absolutely huge, and the soldier was small for even a Vietnamese. The cold barrel of a pistol against the back of his head made him reconsider leaving his place in the semicircle that had been formed before the large rock. The fish nets had been spread out behind the rock just in case they were needed. Now that the lieutenant saw the snake up close, she wondered if the fine nets would be effective.

Private Dong Bec swallowed hard. He had trapped many animals for zoos and private citizens during his life, but he had never even heard about a reticulated python as big as the snake on the rock. He had traveled fifty miles as a young boy to see a python that had been captured in the rice fields west of Hanoi, but that snake had been only twenty-one feet long and much skinnier than the one he was looking at. The wet skin contrasting against the dry rock made her look even *bigger*. He knew the fish nets wouldn't slow her down even a second if she decided on going back into the river. The only way to capture her would be to have the whole platoon grab her and stretch her out so that she couldn't use her coils.

Lieutenant Van Pao caught Dong Bec's attention and nodded for him to start moving his capture team in from his side of the rock.

She flicked out her tongue and sensed the air. A pungent ammonia odor forced her to clean her tongue rapidly and sense the air again. She had never sensed the ammonia odor of living animals as strongly as she was now experiencing. One time she had crawled into a herd of wild pigs, and an ammonia odor had reached her when several of the pigs urinated at the same time, but this was much stronger. She turned her head and sensed the upriver direction, and the same odor reached her. She raised her football-sized brain cavity and sensed with her tongue the green jungle wall behind her, and again the strong ammonia odor. The only direction that was free of the smell was directly over the river. She started to slowly slide toward the river, not alarmed, just very cautious because of the new smell.

Dong Bec saw her start to move toward the water and knew that once she had even a portion of her mass in the fast-moving river, she'd be free. It would be suicide to get into the water with her; once she decided to, she could move very fast. He yelled for the rest of the platoon to follow and ran out on the warm rock in his bare feet.

She sensed the vibrations but ignored the threat of the small beast running toward her on her rock. She continued slipping toward the water, not really in a hurry, just moving in that direction with the majority of her mass still coiled in a large, three-foot-high pile.

Dong Bec reached down and grabbed her head right behind her jaws. He had underestimated the effect the water had on her hide, and his hands slipped as she flexed her muscles and pulled three feet of her body through his grip before he realized what was happening. She turned her head and instantly bit down on the NVA soldier's forearm.

Dong Bec screamed.

Lieutenant Van Pao saw what was happening and yelled for the rest of the platoon to run and assist the trapper, who was himself rapidly becoming trapped. The python, uncoiling from her sun basking, thrashed her coils against the soldier. She had the bite she needed on her prey, and now it was only a matter of starting to coil around it and remove the air from the ammonia-reeking animal's lungs.

"Help him!" The lieutenant screamed. She saw the whole platoon standing in shock, watching the snake coil around their comrade. Lieutenant Van Pao removed her pistol from its holster at her side and fired a round over their heads. "I will start shooting to kill!"

She meant every word. She was not going to report back to Division that she had lost a man to a snake that she had been trying to capture.

Dong Bec screamed again, but this time it came from the very pit of his stomach as he felt the first coil wrap around his leg and cold water touch his ankle. The python was pushing him into the river.

The platoon reacted to the wrenching scream and attacked the snake in unison. The platoon sergeant found her tail and started pulling back on it, and slowly they had enough of her stretched out so that seven men could grab hold and lift ten feet of her off the rock. Too late, she realized what was happening to her, and before she could release her prey and escape, another ten feet of her body was lifted up in a nearly straight line and held off the rock by the ammonia-scented creatures. She was losing her traction; there was nothing to pull against.

Dong Bec fell down on the rock, bleeding profusely from his left forearm. He was mumbling a Buddhist prayer that he had not recited since he had become a Communist.

"Good! You have her!" Lieutenant Van Pao ran over to the line of soldiers and smiled.

"Right now I don't know who has who, Lieutenant!" The platoon sergeant released his hold on the python's tail, and immediately the short, two-foot length tried wrapping itself around the next man in line, whose eyes bulged in fright.

"Hold on!" Van Pao said, as she looked around for the large burlap rice bags they had brought along to put the snake in. She had had two of the bags sewn together and double lined, just in case. The lieutenant was very glad for this extra precaution now that she saw how big the python was close up.

The platoon eased the snake into the sack slowly, ensuring that the head stayed inside the dark bag. They didn't need to worry, because the python had mistaken the sack for a burrow and was cooperating, thinking that she was escaping from them.

"Excellent!" Lieutenant Van Pao was thrilled. "Tie the sack shut and cut a sturdy bamboo pole for carrying her back to camp!"

The lieutenant took a seat on the warm rock and lit up a Russian cigarette. She noticed that her hands were shaking when she held the match against the dry tobacco.

The platoon sergeant and the platoon medic were helping Dong Bec. The medic was bandaging his arm where the python had left rows of teeth marks that would leave deep, permanent scars. The platoon sergeant had removed Dong Bec's shorts and was rinsing them out in the river. The soldier had defecated and urinated during his struggle with the monstrous reptile.

Lieutenant Van Pao smiled and then took a long drag from her cigarette. She now had a tool that could be put to very good use in her business.

Colonel Garibaldi and Corporal Barnett had been locked up in their bamboo cages for the night when the NVA hunting party returned to the compound. The Americans were kept in individual cages, while the more numerous South Vietnamese and Montagnard CIDG prisoners were kept chained up in one of the new longhouses. The small POW camp held only the two American prisoners, but it had room for two more. Colonel Garibaldi's weapons systems officer had been held in the cage across from Barnett until he had died the month before from malaria, and James had spent his first and only night in the cage to the left of Barnett's. The new cage had been built in the exact center of the small American area and was no farther than ten feet from any of the POWs.

Lieutenant Van Pao led the detail carrying their cargo. There were three NVA soldiers at each end of the sagging bamboo pole. Barnett watched and could see that the load they were carrying was heavy. Van Pao stopped in front of the low cage they had just finished building and spoke in rapid Vietnamese to the detail. Two soldiers hopped up on top of the cage and untied the trap door, while the rest of the detail struggled to lift the large rice sack high enough to clear the top of the cage. Barnett smiled as he watched the soldiers struggle. The cargo shifted and moved inside of the sack, which made it even more difficult to handle. As Lieutenant Van Pao glanced over at Barnett and caught him smiling, she flashed a look of pure hate at the American and screamed at her soldiers to hurry up. The sack had finally been placed on top of the cage and the tied end positioned over the open trap door when Private Dong Bec climbed up on the structure, holding a bamboo rod with his good arm. Beaming with pride, he carried his bandaged arm like a baton of honor. He would be the hero for a couple of days in the camp with the rest of the NVA soldiers. Dong Bec loosened the strings that held the sack shut and directed the opening of the bag down into the cage.

Sensing the fresh air, she moved her head out from the safety of her coils and started crawling out of the uncomfortable burrow.

Garibaldi's and Barnett's lungs stopped functioning at exactly the same instant. It looked as if the snake would never stop coming out of the rice sack. She was circling the cage, looking for an opening to escape. Garibaldi had estimated when he was building the cage that it was about fifteen feet long and ten feet wide. Barnett had commented on its chest-high height, and now they knew why; it had been built especially for the python.

"Do you like my new pet?" Lieutenant Van Pao suppressed a giggle. "Well, Spencer Barnett . . . Do you like my pet?"

Spencer heard his own voice answer the woman. "Nice . . . real nice, if you're into that kind of thing."

"I *am,* Spencer. . . . I *love* snakes." She laid her hand against the side of the cage where the snake was circling and tapped the bamboo with her blunt fingernail. "You might have a chance to meet her . . . very soon."

Colonel Garibaldi shuddered. He knew what Sweet Bitch had in the back of her mind. She had interrogated him enough for him to understand her level of reasoning.

The NVA soldiers followed the lieutenant to their mess hall for supper. Barnett could hear her laughing all the way down the trail. The guard positioned in the small shack that overlooked the Americans smiled and lit up a cigarette. Barnett could see that it was taken from a Marlboro pack.

"That fucking thing has to be Kaa's mother!" The colonel watched as she sensed the air between the narrow bamboo bars of her cage. "Jeez! She's got to be thirty-five feet long!" The snake was still circling the cage, trying to find a way out; one long side of the structure as well as a short side had her body pressed up against it, with about a foot of her head and neck just making a turn.

"Who's Kaa?" Barnett found his voice.

"Rudyard Kipling, a British writer, wrote a book about a

boy lost in the jungle, and a huge snake called Kaa sort of adopted him. . . . This thing has got to be his mother!" Garibaldi was amazed. The snake was still clean and shiny from its swim in the river and being in the clean rice sack. She was beautiful.

"What do you think they're going to do with it?" Barnett was afraid to say what he thought.

"I don't know . . . maybe make it a camp pet. . . ." Garibaldi wasn't going to scare the boy and say what was really on his mind.

The conversation stopped when the old Montagnard the NVA used as a runner approached their cages with a small bucket of rice. Barnett pushed his wooden bowl over to the small opening where the old man scooped out two handfuls of the bland food, using his own dirty hand as a spoon. Barnett nodded his thanks, and the old man smiled a near toothless grin and reached into his waistband and removed two small bananas and a wild bird's egg. He patted the egg gently and said something in his native Bru language. Barnett nodded again and smiled.

"I think the old man likes you." Garibaldi spoke from the shadows of his cage. The sun was setting, sending mixed rays of light through the heavy green vegetation.

"I don't know why. . . ." Barnett slipped his arm through the cage and tossed one of the bananas over to the colonel. He had gotten very good at tossing objects, and the banana landed within an inch of the bamboo bars.

"Thanks. . . . " Garibaldi picked up the much-needed fruit that wasn't a normal part of their diet and ate it slowly. "He might feel sorry for you because of the way James harasses you . . . and it might have something to do with his daughter. . . ."

"Who's she?"

"The one James is living with in the village." Garibaldi turned to listen to a noise coming from the South Vietnamese POW compound and continued talking. "I don't think the Bru like it when the NVA take their children and give them to others."

"Well, James treats her like shit." Barnett looked over at the guard, who was ignoring them. Some of the guards didn't care if they talked to each other, but the new ones, directly from units fighting in South Vietnam, would harass them for hours. The NVA soldiers who had been wounded in combat and were recuperating from their wounds were the worst.

The sound of people approaching stopped Barnett and Garibaldi from talking. A squad of NVA soldiers approached in the dim light, dragging a South Vietnamese POW. Garibaldi recognized the man from the first day that he had arrived. He was a second lieutenant from a unit near Da Nang, who had been captured with some of the survivors from his Ranger platoon.

Barnett sat cross-legged on his mat and watched. The NVA sergeant climbed up on Mother Kaa's cage and opened the trap door. He beckoned for the squad to drag the South Vietnamese officer up on the structure. The man realized what they were going to do and started to put up a struggle. They had him almost to the entrance of the cage when he stopped fighting them and began talking in a very humble tone of voice. Barnett couldn't understand what he was saying, but he guessed that the lieutenant was begging for mercy. The NVA sergeant grunted and cuffed the lieutenant before shoving him into the cage with his foot.

Barnett could not remember a longer night in his life. The lieutenant cried and begged the guard to help him and finally ended up crying a series of long wails each time the reptile touched him. Twice during the night Barnett smelled cigarette smoke coming from behind his cage and guessed that Sweet Bitch was listening to the South Vietnamese officer from the shadows.

It was near dawn when the sounds of shuffling and crying ceased in the dark cage. Barnett could hear the snake slithering over the bamboo matting that lined her cage floor, but no sounds came from the lieutenant.

Dawn revealed an answer to the mystery. The South Vietnamese lieutenant had removed his pants and had torn strips from the legs to make a rope. He had crudely hanged himself—or, more accurately, he had slowly strangled himself with the homemade rope using the bamboo bars.

Barnett looked over at Colonel Garibaldi's cage as soon as the morning light was bright enough to see by and saw that the colonel had also been up all night. "Sir . . . I don't think that I can handle it . . . if . . . if they . . ."

"Me neither, Spencer . . . me neither . . ."

The Air Force colonel couldn't take his eyes off the dead South Vietnamese soldier.

CHAPTER TWO

Project Cherry

Sergeant Arnason could see Woods sitting on top of the bunker. Searching through his pockets for his lighter, he took his time lighting the Kool hanging from his lower lip. Even from where he was standing, he could feel the agony coming from Woods without seeing the man's face. It had been weeks since they had returned from the reconnaissance patrol in the A Shau Valley and the decimation of two of their recon teams.

"Watching the dust, Sergeant?" Lieutenant Reed had exited the bunker from the rear entrance and saw his NCO standing there smoking.

"There's enough of it, isn't there." Arnason looked over at the lieutenant. "The bigger this base camp becomes, the more red dust. . . . That shit is everywhere!"

"It makes you want to go to the field, doesn't it?" Reed tried leaning against the burlap wall in the narrow strip of shade the early-afternoon sun provided.

"Yeah . . ." Arnason kept watching Woods.

"How would you like to go back to the A Shau for a short mission?" Reed tried rushing over the name of the NVA stronghold.

Arnason slowly turned his head away from Woods and looked the lieutenant directly in the eyes. He could feel the fear enter his bowels and felt like defecating, but his face didn't reveal any emotion. "The A Shau?"

"Yes. Brigade has received a highly classified message that concerns us." Lieutenant Reed looked around to see if there was anyone near who could eavesdrop on their conversation before continuing. "One of the CIA listening posts in Laos has monitored a telephone conversation between a POW camp commander and a high-ranking NVA intelligence officer." Reed checked the area around him again for people. "Do you remember the seismic-intrusion detectors we planted?"

"How can I forget?" Arnason looked back over to where Woods was sitting. The soldier hadn't changed his position.

"It seems that the NVA have found six of them, but they can't locate the second set . . . the set your team planted."

"Thanks . . . We did try to hide them." Arnason was trying to be sarcastic.

"I hope you didn't camouflage them *too* good, because they want you to go back and retrieve them."

It took a couple of seconds for what the lieutenant had said to sink into Arnason's mind and take precedence in his thoughts. His voice thickened, and the words came out in a jumble. "Are yuh . . . you trying to tell me those motherfuckingstaffbastards . . . after I lost five men dead and two still in the hospital . . . James and Barnett missing . . . Are you telling me they now want me to go back there and *retrieve* those fucking electronic boxes?" Arnason could feel that he was about to lose his temper and fought within himself to regain control. "Three weeks ago—*three weeks!*— those supersecret boxes were *so* damned important! Now they want them back!" Arnason lit another Kool with shaking hands. "Fuck them!"

"Sergeant! I was in *command* of those teams. . . . Don't you think that I feel the loss too?"

"Look at what it did to him!" Arnason nodded in the direction of the distant Woods.

"Who?" Reed couldn't see the soldier sitting on the perimeter bunker.

Arnason curled his lip in contempt. "Woods . . . Have you been to the hospital yet, Lieutenant?"

"I'm going to try and make it there this week. . . . I've been real busy with after-action reports and the debriefings."

"Yeah . . . Tell Kirkpatrick and Sinclair that. . . ." Arnason turned to walk away before he did something stupid. "You were in *command* in the A Shau . . . so *act* like a commander."

"Sergeant! I'm not going to take much more of your bullshit attitude!" Reed exercised his officership. "I'm doing the *best* that I can do! Someone has to fill out the *paperwork*, and you haven't seen me volunteering for it!"

The officer did have a point. He was young and was trying. "Sorry about that, Lieutenant. . . . You're right . . . you're trying to do your best."

"All right . . . let's drop it." Reed's face had turned red. "The mission to the A Shau is going to be quick. We'll be briefed this afternoon, and the insertion is planned for first light in the morning. The plan is simple: Your team will be inserted under a heavy escort of gunships, both Hueys and fast movers. You're to locate the sensors and destroy them."

"Destroy?" Arnason fought back his anger.

"Yes. The sensors have an antitilt device in them, so it's just a matter of locating them and jiggling them a little with an entrenching tool. . . ."

"Simple as that?" Arnason lit his third Kool. "Don't forget, *sir* . . . we *camouflaged* them, so finding the *exact* spot where each one of them is buried is going to be difficult, not simple."

"Sergeant, I was briefed by the brigade commander, *personally*! There's much more to this mission than meets the eye. I've told you all that you need to know. Believe me, it's very important that the NVA doesn't locate the sensors first."

"My team is sort of new." Arnason made the statement to remind the lieutenant that his team hadn't been tested even with a short patrol. "Sinclair is still in the hospital, and it looks as if he's going to be sent back to the States. . . . I've been loaned Simpson, but he's fighting like hell to get off a recon team and stay back in the rear to run his drug ring. . . ."

"You're not being fair, Arnason!" Reed flexed his jaws. "There's no *proof* Simpson is selling drugs!"

Arnason answered the lieutenant with his eyes. He wasn't going to honor the officer's totally ignorant statement with words. The lieutenant knew as well as he did that Private Tousaint Simpson was *the* drug dealer in the An Khe base camp. Lieutenant Reed averted his eyes, and Arnason continued talking. "And this new man . . . Lee San Ko . . . looks promising, but he's going to have to be shaken out first."

"This will be a good mission for him." Reed felt that the subject had turned in his favor. He had personally assigned the new man to Arnason's team. Sergeant Lee San Ko was a full-blooded Chinese American who had come from Hong Kong with his family as a small child. The man was a martial arts expert and had trained in reconnaissance back in the States and Panama. He was very promising and was being groomed as a team leader to replace Sergeant Fitzpatrick, who had been killed in the A Shau Valley.

"You say this is a hot mission?" Arnason's professional side took control as he stuffed his personal emotions away somewhere deep where they wouldn't get in the way.

"Very." Reed acted sure of himself.

"Are you coming along?"

"Not this time." The recon platoon leader had seen bloodshed on his first mission and wasn't thrilled anymore with the idea of going out on long-range recon patrols. He could find plenty to do to keep himself busy back in the brigade base area, and there would be enough missions for him leading combined teams.

Arnason nodded his head in agreement. He saluted the officer and started walking away. "We'll be ready in the morning."

The smell of fried rice filled the indigenous commando mess hall where Master Sergeant McDonald took most of his meals. He sat by himself in deep thought and played with each forkful of food before putting it in his mouth. He was very hungry, but his mind was occupied reviewing the message the Recondo School had received the night before. He had spent the whole night over at the Special Forces headquarters G-3 office reviewing anything he could find on North Vietnamese Army activity in the A Shau Valley and neighboring Laos. He knew a great deal already about the area because of his assignment with Project Cherry, which operated out of Command and Control North, a SOG unit.

McDonald unconsciously rubbed his chest and side while he thought about his assignment with the top-secret project. He could feel the heavy scar tissue through the material of his camouflaged fatigues. An old fear released itself from the dark brain tissue he normally could keep locked up. He could remember everything in vivid detail: the jungle smells and the cool layer of dead bamboo leaves on the ground. McDonald blinked and shoved a forkful of fried rice in his mouth, but the mental vision would not go away. He heard the voices of the searching North Vietnamese and felt the fear deepen. The sound of returning helicopters eased the fear for a second, and then the heavy thuds coming from a Chinese-made 12.7mm machine gun brought the fear back again with an even greater intensity.

"You all right, Mac?"

McDonald blinked his eyes and saw one of the school cadre standing near his table with a tray of food in his hands. "Yeah . . . sure!" He could feel the sweat dripping off his chin and used his arm to wipe it off. The mess hall was cool inside, and there was no visible reason for him to be sweating so hard.

"You sure?"

"Yes . . . I must be having a slight touch of fever . . . malaria." McDonald tried smiling and failed. He covered the attempt by placing his fork in his mouth. The other sergeant gave him a strange look. There was nothing on the fork.

The vision came back the instant the man left. He could feel the blood soaking through his sweat-stained jacket. An

army ant ran across his face and stopped next to his nose
before deciding that he was too big to haul back to the main
body of ants. He blinked his eyes, unable to move. The
sound of a small snake sliding over the bamboo leaves
reached him, and then the loud noise of the machine gun
drowned out the jungle sounds. The weapon was close to
where he lay on the jungle floor. He guessed that it was
within a hundred meters. The last burst from the antiaircraft
machine gun was answered by a blast of intense heat.
McDonald felt the wave of extremely hot air pass over him,
and then the heat was sucked back in the direction it had
come from. A fast mover had dropped a napalm bomb on
the machine gun position.

The jungle became quiet. He liked it. It was better than
having to listen to the NVA searching for him or the Chinese
machine gun. He liked the quiet better. The first scream
reached him only seconds after the explosion, but in his
confused state of mind it seemed like minutes, or maybe a
couple of centuries. The NVA gun crew was being roasted
alive from the napalm that had stuck to their clothes and
skin. He lay under the bamboo and thought about the sound
of the screams and decided that he liked it. They had had no
mercy for the South Vietnamese prisoners of war.

McDonald blinked. He felt the fork dig into his lower lip.
He had missed his mouth.

The Project Cherry assault team had reached the edge of
the prisoner-of-war camp and was under intense ground fire.
McDonald knew that he couldn't hesitate or the NVA would
kill their POWs before allowing for them to be repatriated by
the team. A light machine gun opened fire to his left, and he
gave the command to take it out of action with an LAW
missile. His forty-man team was extremely well trained. A
slight hand movement from him would send a squad of men
maneuvering instantly. He had spent three months training
day and night with the prisoner snatch team, and they were
good; they were the best.

McDonald had no way of knowing the NVA had moved a
battalion of regulars to a night rest site a few hundred

meters away from the NVA POW camp. His team was destroying the camp guards, and they were within a few feet of the South Vietnamese POWs when the first assault hit his flank and stopped his progress cold. The Project Cherry group fought valiantly to the man. There was no quarter asked, nor was any given. McDonald's vision became even clearer as he recalled running through the center of the POW camp with the remaining seven men from his team. He saw again for the hundred billionth time the row of South Vietnamese prisoners tied to the horizontal narrow wooden planks that had been propped up off the ground with small homemade bamboo sawhorses. The prisoners' arms had been stretched out over their heads and chained to the planks. A hole had been cut through each one of the planks where the POW's buttocks were located. McDonald could see from the large piles of feces piled under the planks, that some of the prisoners had been chained to their wooden bed boards for quite a while. The NVA guards had cut each one of the POWs' throats.

McDonald and his men had run directly into the NVA company that had taken up a blocking position. He had been hit five times, by an AK-47 firing a short burst. The seven commandos had fallen like cut wheat. None of them had had a chance to even fire their weapons. McDonald had taken a round through both cheeks that missed his jaws and teeth. The massive bleeding from the wound had made it look as if half of his head had been blown off and had saved him from a coup-de-grace round from the NVA officer's pistol. The other seven commandos weren't so lucky. McDonald could hear each one of the rounds thud against flesh as he lay on the ground slowly bleeding to death. The NVA officer barked a command, and the blocking troops formed a skirmish line and moved off to sweep through the camp for other survivors.

McDonald had dropped his fork and was staring directly at the side of the mess-hall wall. His vision totally possessed him. The NCO who had stopped by his table earlier had kept his eye on the senior sergeant and could see that the soldier was having some kind of mental problem. McDonald was highly respected in the Recondo School, and the sergeant didn't want whatever was happening to the senior NCO to go too far. He left his seat and headed toward the commandant's office for help.

McDonald had crawled away from the pile of dead commandos toward a thick clump of bamboo. Escape was all that he could think about. If he had been functioning with a normal mind, he would have given up, but after seeing what the NVA had done to the POWs, he knew that he had to try to escape before they returned and discovered that he was still alive. The bamboo leaves on the ground felt cool to his touch in the shade. He piled as many leaves as he could scrape up against his body without moving too much. His left arm didn't work, and even though he had told his body that he wanted to get on his feet, nothing responded as it should have. McDonald spent a couple of minutes trying to reach the transponder attached to his web gear and pushed the rubber-coated switch. A signal was instantly emitted and brought a near-instant reaction.

A battalion of infantry had been placed on standby alert in case the Project Cherry team ran into a larger force than they could handle. The signal from McDonald's transponder had been prearranged. A flight of gunships was circling nearby and began their attack pattern. Three flights of F-4 jets that had been on call to the FAC pilot began their attack. The first infantry company was already loaded and waiting on their slicks for the command to go. Everything was automatic, responding to the signal from the transponder. McDonald had told the command center that his force was lost and that they should attack his location. And so the battle changed for the third time that day. The NVA battalion was encircled and destroyed almost to the man. McDonald was found by one of the companies in its search of the POW camp for NVA survivors. Even though the Project Cherry team had been wiped out, with McDonald being the only survivor, the end results of the battle looked very impressive on paper: 62 friendly troops killed in action, 21 POWs murdered, and 51 friendly troops wounded, against 423 North Vietnamese killed and no wounded.

"Sergeant McDonald?"

He heard his name being called from far away and ignored it.

"Sergeant McDonald?" The school commandant reached over and gently shook the master sergeant's shoulder.

He blinked and his eyes focused.

"I need to talk with you over in my office after supper." The lieutenant colonel grinned when he saw that the sergeant was all right. "Can you make it in, say, fifteen minutes?"

McDonald wiped the sweat off his face. "Yes sir . . ." He blinked again. "I feel like shit."

"It may be a fever coming back."

"Yeah . . . a fever." McDonald got to his feet and felt his legs flex and then hold. He was back again. The dark cells in his brain closed their doors. The room became bright, and he was functioning once more. "Oh . . . sir!"

"Yes?" The colonel stopped.

"I'll take that assignment." McDonald licked his lips. His mouth was dry.

"Good! I can't think of a more qualified man to lead a prisoner snatch operation." The commandant's voice lowered. "You read the message and understand what must be done?" Anger underscored each word. "And my being a black officer makes it even that much more important. . . . I might sound selfish, but that motherfu—" He swallowed the cussword. "That *traitor* has got to be either eliminated or captured!"

"I could care less about Mohammed James." McDonald picked up his tray. "It's the boy, Spencer Barnett, I care about."

"Whatever your reason for going . . . just remember, you have anything you want for support. Just name it."

"Thanks, sir."

"Come on . . . we've got a lot to talk about before you leave for Da Nang, where you'll be assembling your team. . . ."

* * *

Woods heard the person approaching from his rear. He sat looking out over the barbed wire. Time was supposed to make the hurt go away, but it was getting worse every day; he knew he was going crazy.

"David . . . yo!"

Woods recognized his sergeant's voice but still sat looking out over the perimeter.

"We've got a mission!" Arnason tried sounding cheerful. "We're going to get our asses away from this RAMF shit!"

Woods spoke a single word through his teeth: "Where?"

"How about . . ." Arnason let the suspense build. "Let's say the A Shau?"

Woods whirled around on his sandbag seat. "When?"

"Would tomorrow morning be early enough for you?" Arnason knew what Woods was thinking, but he didn't care. This was the first time since they had returned from the mission on which Barnett had been taken prisoner that Woods showed any sign of being alive.

"Tonight!"

"Sorry, you'll have to wait." Arnason shook his head. "And would you believe that we're going back to the *exact* location?"

Woods frowned. "Why?" He became instantly suspicious.

"The brass want us to destroy the sensors we put in along the trail."

"Destroy them!" Woods started breathing hard. "Destroy them after what it *cost* to put them in?"

"The brass have their reasons, David. . . . *We obey orders!*" Arnason hesitated and then added, "Besides, it gives us a chance to go back and search the area again. . . ."

"Yes." Woods spoke the word with so much emotion that the sound almost took shape and could be seen hanging in the dusty air.

The weather was perfect. It was as if some unseen force had smiled on the mission the First Cavalry Division's recon team had been assigned. The valley was sparkling in the sunlight, and there wasn't a trace of the deadly fog that had been there during their first mission in the A Shau. Arnason and Woods weren't fooled by the tranquil, lush green foliage; they knew that death lived down under the trees.

A platoon of gunships prepped the area that they were inserting with rockets and then banked to the north end of the valley to wait for a flight of fast movers to drop their loads of five-hundred-pound bombs. Woods could see the tiny L-19, which carried the forward air controller, bounce in the strong updrafts coming from the valley floor. The Special Forces A-camp sat like a boil in the southern end of the green, NVA-controlled valley.

Arnason scooted forward until his legs were hanging out of the open doors of the helicopter. He tried scanning the skies for Puff the Magic Dragon, an AC-47 fixed-wing aircraft that had been modified to fire miniguns out of its port windows. The aircraft could stay on station almost forever, giving a tremendous hail of fire to locations on the ground. The aircraft had also been equipped to drop flares, but it was the firepower Arnason wanted in case they ran into trouble. He couldn't see the plane, but he was sure that it was circling nearby. He felt much better going in this time, compared with their last walk-in mission. He had a lot of support, and the mission was going to be a quick one. The team had only to locate the six sensors, destroy them, and be extracted. He didn't plan on being on the ground more than an hour.

The copilot beckoned that they were getting lined up to approach the landing zone that had been created by dropping five-hundred-pound bombs with thirty-six-inch-long fuses attached to them so that the blast would level trees and underbrush. It worked well for small one- or two-aircraft LZs.

Arnason recognized the familiar finger of rock sticking out from the side of the mountain where they had spent the night during their first mission. He felt a shiver ripple down his back, but it was too late to stop now. Sergeant Lee San Ko leaned forward on his side of the Huey and located the LZ; he tapped Simpson, who jumped at the touch, and pointed down. Woods was ready: he had his CAR-15 slung over his shoulder with the thirty-round magazine inserted. He was hoping the landing zone would be hot; he needed to kill some NVA soldiers to release the hate that had built up inside of him.

The chopper touched the side of the mountain, and the team bailed out. Arnason knew exactly where he was within seconds of touching the ground and gave hand signals to direct his team until the choppers pulled away. The Air Force jets were working over the mountainside a thousand meters to the north.

She growled. The cave protected her from the bomb blasts, but she didn't like the extremely loud noise so close to her. The sound in the distance had always meant plenty of food, but so close to her cave it made her angry. She turned her head to one side and roared her anger. A cloud of dust rolled into the wide opening as if in answer to her growl. She coughed and swatted at the fine particles of gray dust the bombs had created outside of her den. She felt the movement within her womb and rolled more to one side to allow her unborn cubs to adjust their positions within her. One of the bombs landing outside of her cave dispersed the rib cage and skull from a human skeleton against the low cliff that ran from the thick jungle up the path to the entrance of her private domain. A GI dog tag flew through the air and lodged itself in a crack. It sparkled in the sunlight, and if you could read English, a short message could be read as to the owner.

> FILLMORE
> BILLY-BOB
> 371420265
> O NEG
> PENTECOSTAL

The loud noise from the bombs stopped as suddenly as it had started. She stood and hobbled to the entrance of her cave. The dust had settled, and the bright sunlight sparkled

off her beautiful striped hide, all except for the large black
spot on her hip that had been burned. She would have been a
fantastic trophy for any big-game hunter, weighing in at over
780 pounds, an enormous weight for an Asian tiger.

She roared her anger again, and this time the rest of the
jungle heard her and showed their respect by becoming
quiet.

Woods ran straight ahead and took up a fighting position
near the edge of a bomb crater. Arnason passed him and
headed in the direction of the trail. He had a little difficulty
locating the first seismic-intrusion detector, but after that it
was fairly easy locating the rest, because he remembered
how far apart they were. Woods worked frantically with his
entrenching tool, digging up the sensors and flipping them
over to activate the destruction devices. He recalled how
heavy they were carrying them up the mountain and was
glad that they didn't have to haul them out again.

The Special Forces captain sat in his command bunker
and watched the lights first flash on, telling him that the
sensor had been activated, and then flash off, signaling that
the instrument had been destroyed. He waited until each one
of the devices had flashed its message on the receiver in his
A-camp, and then he called back the number that had been
broadcast to his headquarters. He understood why the secret
devices had to be destroyed, but at the same time he was
very unhappy about it, because the sensors had provided him
and his team with a number of early warnings regarding
enemy movement, just in the few weeks they had been
working.

Arnason located the last sensor and pointed for Simpson
to dig it up and activate it. Sergeant Lee San Ko worked
over the surrounding jungle with his eyes. He radiated an
impressive sense of calmness under pressure. Arnason was
well pleased so far with the NCO. He keyed his radio and
called for the slicks to return and pick up his team. They had

accomplished their mission. He waved Lee San Ko and Simpson back to him and looked for Woods. Arnason shifted his position to the opposite side of the trail and looked both ways for Woods and still couldn't locate him.

Arnason turned to the junior sergeant and whispered, "Where's Woods?"

Lee San Ko pointed with his rifle barrel down the trail. "He was going in that direction the last time I saw him."

Arnason knew.

Woods moved down the trail in a low crouch, but he still maintained his speed. He wanted to get as far away from the recon team as possible before Arnason discovered him missing. He knew that technically he was going AWOL, but he didn't care. He was going to find Spencer Barnett or die in the process. He knew that he couldn't go on living with the memory of leaving his friend behind haunting him every day and night, especially after he had promised Spencer that he would never leave him alive out in the jungle.

Sergeant Arnason knew that he had only a few minutes to catch up to Woods before the extraction helicopters arrived. He hoped that Woods had stayed on the trail and wasn't moving too fast. He himself was running with little regard as to any chance meeting with NVA soldiers, banking on the air strikes' having cleared the immediate area of any enemy for him. Arnason just caught a glimpse of Woods's back as the soldier turned a slight bend in the trail. He ran harder.

Woods heard the footfalls and turned with his CAR-15 to meet the threat. He was hoping that it would be NVA, but he knew instantly that Arnason had figured out what he was planning to do.

Woods hissed the words. "Get away!"

Arnason dived and tackled Woods just above his knees. The pair rolled into the thick underbrush. Woods struggled, but his CAR-15 and pack hindered him. Arnason grabbed Woods under his jaw and forced his head back against the thick plants on the ground.

"You're coming back now!" Arnason growled the words. "No questions asked!"

Woods realized that the game was up and nodded his head in agreement.

"And no more of this shit! You hear?" Arnason was angry. "I like Barnett too! But this is not the way to find him!"

Woods's eyes flashed his anger, and he tried talking with Arnason's fingers squeezing his cheeks. His voice sounded muffled. "I made a promise."

"Let's get back. . . . I've already called for extraction." Arnason ended the conversation

The run back to the edge of the landing zone seemed a thousand times longer than it had going for both of the men. Arnason could see the slick making its approach and signaled for Simpson and Lee San Ko to load up first. He kept himself within arm's length of Woods. The chopper's skids were starting to lift off the rocks when Arnason hopped on board and took hold of Woods's web gear. The look in the sergeant's eyes told the soldier not to try to jump back down on the ground. Woods sighed and leaned back against the nylon webbing of the seat.

The Special Forces captain stood in the clearing inside of his A-camp with the hand flare uncapped, ready to fire. He waited until the slick was passing over his camp and rammed his open palm against the bottom of the blue star cluster.

Arnason could see the burst off to his right side and looked down at the small dot on the ground. He gave the captain a thumbs-up sign and smiled.

The tigress had watched the two humans wrestling on the edge of the trail and was just about ready to attack when they stopped and started running back down the trail. She knew that her maimed hip would prevent her from catching either one of them and growled her disappointment. She started a slow hobble down the trail, knowing that every time the loud sounds came to the jungle there was always something dead that was good to eat.

CHAPTER THREE

Black Cong

The old Montagnard sat under the shady overhang of the thatched roof of the longhouse and mixed another pot of rice wine. He dipped in water from the jug his eldest grandson had carried up from the river and then added a handful of husked rice. The wine was being fermented for a special ceremony in honor of Tang Lie, the devil spirit that had taken possession of their village through the North Vietnamese. He mumbled enticing chants under his breath as he prepared the wine, trying to get Tang Lie interested in the intoxicating drink. The tribe was hoping that they could get Tang Lie drunk and then lead him from the village so that their god, Ae Die, would return and bring happiness back to the mountain community.

The girl began to cry very softly, but the old man could still hear her through the matting that covered the end of the community house. She was his youngest daughter and his favorite one. He heard the American soldier begin grunting like a pig and knew that he had mounted her again. The old Montagnard threw in a double handful of rice and slowly stirred the large pot of wine. He watched the tiny bubbles rise to the top and begged Tang Lie to accept his humble gift and give the black American soldier the disease that slowly rots away a man's body. He added another handful of rice and asked that the leprosy start with the man's sex organ.

The North Vietnamese soldier looked up in the sky for aircraft before running the short distance from Lieutenant Van Pao's office to the longhouse where the black American lived with his Montagnard woman. He hated going to get the American, because every time he saw the man his jealousy burned his throat. The American was the only one allowed to have a woman all to himself.

The old man saw the soldier coming and removed any expression of hate from his face. The Vietnamese thought the mountain people were dumb, so he would act dumb for them. He added another handful of rice to his wine. Tang Lie would be very happy: the wine was strong and would make the evil one's head hurt.

The NVA runner pushed the bamboo curtain aside and saw the naked man lying next to the young girl. "Come! The lieutenant wants to talk to you!"

"Get the fuck out of here!" James pointed his finger at the soldier but made no attempt to cover his nakedness. He enjoyed teasing the North Vietnamese by exposing his large penis; it was one of the few things he could do to show his superiority over them.

"Come now!" The soldier left the longhouse angry. He wanted to kill the American pig, slowly.

Lieutenant Van Pao sat behind her makeshift bamboo desk with her hands folded in front of her. She twisted her lip and stared directly into Barnett's eyes. "What am I going to do with you, Spencer? You refuse to cooperate. . . . You taunt the soldiers of the People's Army. You are *not* a good boy!"

Barnett sat on the bamboo pole that had been erected in her office and struggled to balance himself. The pole was designed not as a seat, but for a man to hang from upside down. The guards on each side of Barnett held him up by holding him under his armpits. He had been tied to the pole in the worst torture position of all. The two-inch bamboo rod had been placed behind his knees, and his forearms were pulled forward under the bar and tied at his wrists. A thin parachute cord was tied around his ankles and pulled tight and tied behind his back and around his neck. Once the guards let go of him, he would roll off the top of the bar and hang below it, with all of his weight falling on his knee joints. If he tried relaxing his legs, the parachute cord would start to strangle him.

"Please! Please, cooperate with us and I can have you untied. . . . Oh, Spencer Barnett, you have served your country well!" She smiled when James walked into the room and stood next to the doorjamb behind Barnett where he couldn't be seen. "Why can't you be sensible like Mohammed James and help us?"

"Fuck you, Sweet Bitch."

She flinched. The nickname the POWs called her behind her back always angered her, not because of what it meant but because it showed a lack of respect for her as a soldier and an NVA officer.

"Come on, Spence . . ." James stepped forward so Barnett could see his smiling face. "It's not that bad . . . you might even get a woman."

Barnett didn't answer James. He glared at him, and with his eyes he told his ex-teammate what he would like to do to him.

"Now, now, Spence . . ." James huffed and smiled, using only one side of his mouth. "Don't you remember the last time you got uppity?"

"Enough, Mohammed James!" Van Pao wasn't going to give up her authority as the senior interrogator of prisoners. "I will handle him."

Spencer sucked as much spit as he could from his dry mouth and looked over at James. The spit hit the black soldier under his left eye. Barnett smiled.

"You!" James took a step forward and was stopped by the guard holding Spencer's left arm. "You're dead!"

"Spencer . . . this is your last chance! Tell me where you buried the sensors, and you'll be cut free. . . ." She lit a

Marlboro and blew the smoke at the prisoner. "If not . . ."
She shrugged her shoulders. "We haven't had a prisoner die
in a long time . . . not since the South Vietnamese lieutenant
committed suicide."

Barnett took a deep breath, knowing what was coming
next. It was going to be the last easy breath he would take
for quite a while.

The guards released Spencer's arms, causing the prisoner
to fall backward, almost making a complete revolution
around the pole. The pain was instant. He rocked back and
forth under the smooth rod, which bent under his weight.
The yokes at each end of the pole vibrated but remained
upright. That was the good thing about bamboo: it always
gave under pressure from the elements and never broke.
Barnett recalled what Colonel Garibaldi had told him about
being flexible. When he had first been interrogated, he tried
not to yell or scream, but the colonel had assured him that he
would last longer without telling them what they wanted to
know if he screamed as loud as he could.

Lieutenant Van Pao strolled over to where Spencer hung
and gently caressed the bare soles of his feet with her split
bamboo rod. She walked around him for a couple of minutes, humming softly, and then she swung the bamboo version of a cat-o'-nine-tails hard so that the split rod landed on
the soft inner soles of Spencer's feet. The pain behind his
knees was forgotten as his feet burst apart in pain. Spencer
bit his lip, even though the colonel had told him to start
screaming the instant they touched him. He would try to
hold back for just a little while.

"Well, he's going to be a *brave* boy today." She lashed out
with the rod again and again, until she heard the first
whimper from the young man's throat.

"Let me have a swing. . . ." Mohammed James held out
his hand for the bamboo rod. Van Pao hesitated and then
smiled. She gave the switch to James and spoke rapidly to
one of the guards in Vietnamese.

Spencer was gasping for air. The pause in the lashes
against his feet let the pain flash up his legs.

James noticed the bulge in Barnett's black pajama pants where the teenager's testes were and lowered his aim. The blow was so hard that it rocked Spencer halfway around the pole.

The old Montagnard heard the blond boy's screams from his seat on the porch. He stopped adding water to his rice wine and looked over toward the building where the female Vietnamese tortured the prisoners and occasionally one of the villagers. He had been the headman of the village until the North Vietnamese soldiers had come. He had spent a couple of very unpleasant days in the darkened room.

Colonel Garibaldi heard Spencer's scream and felt like crying. He watched Mother Kaa sleeping in her cage and mumbled to himself. "Please . . . talk, Spencer! Tell them every damn thing you know! Talk . . . talk . . . *talk*." He started crying.

The old Montagnard struggled to his feet. The cool weather was making his joints hurt all of the time. His eyes were getting so bad that he was blind as soon as it got dusk outside; even with a full moon, he was sufficiently incapacitated to need one of his grandsons to lead him to the men's place behind the village, if he had to go at night. He knew what he must do; a Bru chief did not sit idly by and allow the evil spirit, Tang Lie, to bring so much pain to his village. He was still the chief of the Bru.

Colonel Garibaldi looked over at his wooden cross and started praying for Christ to intervene and stop the boy's pain.

Spencer passed out.

"He isn't lasting as long as he used to. . . ." She gently tapped the bamboo whip against her leg and could feel the sting through her khaki pants. She stopped hitting herself.

One of her soldiers appeared in the doorway. "Lieutenant! There is a call for you in the radio bunker!"

She nodded her head and started for the door. She turned

and looked at James, who was watching Barnett's face. "Mohammed?"

James looked up at the officer with an expression of pure pleasure. "Yes?"

"You were too busy to notice...." She held up the half-dozen Polaroid photographs of him beating Barnett that her guard had just taken and fanned them out in her hand. "This is what we call in the intelligence community... *insurance*."

"Keep them! I could give a fuck less...Lieutenant!" James spat out the words.

She left, and all but one of the guards followed her. She shivered when her back felt the warm sunlight touch it, not from the warmth but from her thoughts of Mohammed James. He was a very sick man.

Spencer had forced his eyes open and saw the photographs in Lieutenant Van Pao's hand. The pain coming from his feet, buttocks, and testes was excruciating and blended together as one great force. He swallowed hard and shivered.

"James...I am going to kill you...." The words were spoken so softly that James barely heard him.

"You're not going to do shit, honkie!" James kicked Spencer's bruised buttocks, sending the POW swinging back and forth, as he left the darkened room.

Mohammed James walked down the jungle trail with Spencer Barnett's CAR-15 slung over his right shoulder. The short version of the M-16 rifle was perfectly designed for the thick jungles of the highlands. The telescoping stock could be pulled out and the weapon selector switch placed on semiautomatic, or else the weapon could be used as a compact, fully automatic submachine gun. James smiled to himself as he walked between the NVA company commander and the unit's first sergeant. He was recalling the first time Spencer Barnett had seen him carrying the weapon. His ex-teammate had literally thrown himself against the bars of his cage and screamed curses at him. It served the uppity white trash right to have the weapon taken away from him. Sergeant McDonald had no right giving Woods and Barnett their own CAR-15s after they had graduated from the Recondo School in Nha Trang. He had graduated too, and with honors! That was the way it was with white people: they always took care of each other and shit on the black and colored people of the world! James's smile changed to a full-mouthed grin. Who had the CAR-15 now?

The North Vietnamese column he was part of moved at a casual pace down the jungle road that would have been a trail in a more developed country. NVA engineers had built the road running next to the Rao Lao River to link up with Highway 547 in South Vietnam, cutting the A Shau Valley in half and providing high-speed access to the prized city of Da Nang. Groups of NVA soldiers passed James's unit riding bicycles on their return trips to the NVA supply depots in Laos. The NVA modified the bikes to carry huge loads of ammunition and supplies to their troops in the south by removing the seat and placing the load where the man would normally ride. The soldier would walk next to the bike and steer it using a modified bar across the handlebars.

James had learned a great deal about the NVA in just the short couple of weeks he had agreed to work with them against American units. The NVA traveled mostly at night down well-used trails and roads. The jungle was used only to get into and out of major command or supply areas in the south. The American units spent almost all of their time humping through the heavy jungle sounding like an old steam engine as they hacked their way through the virgin terrain. The NVA were *never* taken by surprise if the American unit was larger than a squad. James wondered how much the American intelligence people would pay him for what he knew about NVA small-unit operations; it could probably change the results of the Vietnam War.

The North Vietnamese commander stopped his company and gave orders for his men to fill their canteens and eat. James found himself a comfortable spot to sit next to a large tree and removed his nylon backpack. He opened a side

pocket and took out a can of potatoes and beef. Everything
James wore was authentic American equipment, down to his
underwear. He was supplied with gear that had been taken
off American dead and POWs. The only thing that James did
not wear was camouflage paint, and there was a reason for
that: the NVA wanted the fact that he was a black man to be
very obvious to anyone they encountered once they reached
the Laotian–South Vietnamese border.

James leaned back against the tree and ate his can of C-
rations alone. The NVA soldiers stayed away from him, and
only the first sergeant or the company commander would
even bother talking to him. James liked it when the sergeant
gave him his orders, because the man spoke almost letter-
perfect English—in fact, the North Vietnamese spoke English better than he did.

Sweat rolled down in his eyes, and he used the back of his
hand to wipe it away. He started thinking of home, back in
Detroit, Michigan, where he had been raised in a white-built
ghetto that had been designed to contain the black people
and keep them all together, below 8 Mile Road in the city.
The whites had always treated black people like shit. The
ghetto projects where his mother had found them an apart-
ment were new when they moved in, but the whites who
controlled everything in Detroit refused to give the black
people good jobs, and so they were forced to tear the toilets
and sinks out of the apartments and sell them to feed their
families. If a light bulb was screwed into a socket in the
hallway, it was gone within minutes. The halls at night became a battle zone for muggers and dope dealers.

Mohammed James ground his teeth as he thought about
how the white people treated blacks back home in Detroit.
The whites were the ones who had forced his mother to work
long, eighteen-hour days operating a steam press in a white-
owned laundry. She had caught pneumonia during his four-
teenth winter and died. Mohammed chose to live in the
streets, rather than go to the Wayne County Youth Home and
be forced to feed the emotional vampires who worked there
under the protection of the powerful social services organi-

zation. It was on the streets that he had first met the man who became the most powerful influence in his life: Malcolm Pride. James had learned through the popular Black Moslem exactly what his personal calling in life was, and at sixteen years of age, James had become the youngest Death Angel in the United States.

A smile of pride crossed James's face under the jungle tree. He had known from his first Black Moslem secret ceremony for Death Angels what his lifetime vocation was going to be.

Whites were dumb. He remembered cruising down Highway 75, just south of River Rouge, and picking up white teenagers who were running away from home and hitchhiking out to the hippie mecca called California to join communes and fuck all day long. Whites were dumb. It was only a matter of persuading them to get into the van, and then there would be a half-dozen of them pushing and shoving to choose from. It seemed like every intersection of the highway had a group of hippies waiting for rides. He liked the blond ones with the light blue eyes the best. Malcolm had told them that those were the ones who grew up to be the worst white devils, and it was best to kill them early, before they could do harm to the pure black folk.

Whites were dumb. He knew of five white teenagers who would never return to their homes in Detroit from their hippie pilgrimages to California; that was the number of whites it took to become a Death Angel.

Yes, when Malcolm Pride had entered James's life, everything had taken its proper place, and he became very useful to someone. What Mohammed James had never realized, and probably never would, was that his great friend Malcolm Pride had seen in him what even the most incompetent psychologist would have instantly detected: that here was a psychopathic killer who, even had he lived in all-black Africa, would still have killed for pleasure. Knowing this, Malcolm channeled the hate to white people and gave James a cause and a reason to kill by being a Death Angel for the Moslem movement.

The NVA officer spoke sharply now to his junior leaders, and the company started preparing to move out of their break site. There was a noticeable difference in the way the soldiers acted. The lackadaisical attitude of the troops was gone. The soldiers, who had been carrying their weapons by their barrels over their shoulders, now carried the weapons at the ready. James knew they were crossing into South Vietnam's A Shau Valley. Lieutenant Van Pao had briefed him before he left the POW camp that an American battalion had moved into the A Shau, and she was almost sure that it was a unit from the First Cavalry Division, his old outfit.

Mohammed James took his position ten meters out in front of the NVA point element and began earning his keep.

Corporal Barnett lay in the bamboo cage where the guards had left him. He barely moved, and when he did, a groan escaped his throat. The bottoms of his feet were raw, and his arches were so bruised that it would be weeks before he could walk without limping. The blows James had given him across his testicles had caused both genital glands to swell to triple their normal size. His scrotum had been cut and oozed a mixture of blood and other body fluid. There would be scars on Spencer's buttocks when the deep cuts finally healed . . . if he lived.

Colonel Garibaldi kept eyeing Barnett's cage every time he had a chance to pass it or work near the cages. The guards had been instructed to forbid him to administer to the teenager's wounds until after their supper meal, and then they would allow him to stay with him in the cage for only a half-hour. Garibaldi spent the day gathering anything that he might be able to use on Spencer: pieces of cloth for bandages, sticks for splints. He even begged a small bottle of liquid Chinese aspirin off one of the older guards.

The small Montagnard boy reached through the bamboo bars and lifted Spencer's head just enough to pour the thick monkey meat stew down his throat. The effect of the high-protein food was almost immediate on the starving man.

Barnett's eyes fluttered, and his mouth kept moving like that of a small baby when its bottle was removed before it had finished nursing. The boy looked constantly around the cage for any approaching guards. He then pulled a dirty Vietnamese perfume bottle out of his loincloth waistband. He looked back across the pungi stake barrier and saw that his grandfather was watching from the porch. The opium-brewed pain reliever burned and tasted bitter against Spencer's tongue, but the numbing effect of the powerful drug was almost immediate. Spencer felt a hand tugging at the drawstring of his black peasant pants and a sharp pain as the trousers were tugged down, breaking the scabs of his wounds that had dried against the material. The boy worked swiftly, rubbing the salve deep into all of Spencer's wounds. An old Montagnard woman had made the opium-based ointment by boiling the sap down and mixing it with animal fat and jungle plants. The ointment did a number of things to the wounds that enabled Spencer to fall asleep.

The Bru chieftain's grandson slipped the empty perfume bottle back into his waistband and dropped down in the shadows next to Barnett's cage. He was taking a great risk and knew the guard would kill him without question if he was caught near the American soldier, but his grandfather's orders were to be obeyed without fear. The Ae Die liked good deeds, and his grandfather was a close friend of the mountain spirit. He would be protected from evil.

Colonel Garibaldi was shocked to see Spencer awake when he returned from his work detail. He had feared all day long that he would be burying the young soldier when he returned.

Barnett tried smiling, but failed. "Are you working half-days now, Colonel?"

The older man grabbed the bamboo bars and pressed his face up against the smooth fibers. "How are you feeling?" Garibaldi blinked back the tears. Spencer looked so helpless lying on his stomach. "I was a little worried about you this morning."

"I'm a little buzzed. . . ."

"What?" Garibaldi became alarmed.

"One of the Montagnard kids brought me a little jug of what I think was dope. It sure has stopped the pain. . . . And then he rubbed some greasy stuff all over my ass . . ." Spencer wasn't ashamed and continued talking, "and nuts. . . . Whatever it was, it works. The pain is gone."

Colonel Garibaldi could see that Spencer's eyes weren't focusing like they should and figured the Montagnards had drugged the young soldier so that he could rest and start healing. The risks that they took in approaching the American POW cages in bright daylight were tremendous. The colonel turned around slowly, knowing that the guard was watching him, and looked across the pungi stake clearing to where an old Montagnard and a small nine-year-old boy sat watching him from the porch of their longhouse. The American colonel checked to see what the guard was doing and saw that the NVA soldier was reading a letter from home. Garibaldi placed his palms together against his chest and tilted the top half of his body forward in an Oriental sign of great respect to the old man. The boy whispered something in the nearsighted old man's ear, and the Bru chieftain smiled a betel-nut—stained grin and nodded his head in the direction of the Americans.

The squad leader was the first one to sight the American soldier walking down the center of the trail. He blinked his eyes rapidly to clear his vision and confirmed that the man he saw was a black American. The sergeant didn't take the time to wonder what a lone GI was doing walking down a trail deep in NVA-held territory. He waited until the soldier drew near to his hidden position and called out softly, "What in the hell are you doing here?"

James was startled and took a step sideways before catching himself. He spoke loud enough for the NVA point element to hear him. "Man! Am I glad to see you! I got fucking lost!"

"Quiet!" The sergeant lifted up a little higher from his

prone position and looked down the trail in the direction of Laos. "This fucking place is crawling with NVA."

James kept trying to locate the rest of the sergeant's patrol hidden in the jungle, but couldn't even find the man nearest to the NCO. The NVA company had nearly walked into a perfect claymore ambush. "Naw . . . I just came from that way . . ." James pointed down the trail, "and there ain't anything *hostile* for a couple clicks at least."

"Who are you with?" The sergeant remained in his camouflaged position.

"The Cav . . ."

"So are we . . . Second Brigade?"

"No . . . I'm with the First Brigade's Recon Company. . . ."

"Get your ass in here and off the trail." The sergeant waved for James to join him.

The NVA point heard James talking in English and figured that he had run into an American element. The NVA company began maneuvering around the area.

"You're wasting your time on this trail. . . . My recon team has worked this area for the last three days, and we haven't seen any sign of NVA."

"Yeah? We've been out here since last night and are about ready to pull back to the battalion's perimeter." The sergeant automatically nodded his head in the direction the Cavalry unit was bivouacked.

James felt his stomach roll. An American battalion could maul the NVA company he was with in a matter of minutes. "How far?"

The sergeant pulled an ant off his cheek and looked at it before crushing the insect between his fingers. "A couple hundred meters . . . Well, if you just came from that direction and say it's clear, we might as well break this ambush." The sergeant whistled softly and called to his men. A minute passed with the Americans signaling to one another that it was all clear. The squad left the protection of the jungle and eased out onto the trail. James was impressed with how well they were camouflaged and how disciplined they were.

"Man, you've got a good team!" James smiled as he complimented the sergeant. "I didn't even suspect that you were here."

"Thanks; I work hard at keeping my men alive.... We might die in this fucking war, but it won't be because I made a stupid mistake."

"I know whatcha mean." James turned his head away from the NCO so he couldn't see his malignant smile.

The squad worked smoothly, breaking apart the claymore ambush and rolling up the wires to the antipersonnel mines. Within five minutes the ambush site was clean and the men were ready to leave. The sergeant walked silently along the edge of the trail through the old ambush kill zone and signaled for his men to follow him and James. A couple of the men gave James a curious look, but none of them broke silence. There would be plenty of time to ask questions when they got back inside of the battalion's perimeter.

James noticed that there were only seven men in the squad counting the sergeant, which was normal for Vietnam units, considering that men were constantly going on R and R and sick call from the field; most infantry companies operated about thirty percent short.

The cracking sound of the first AK-47 dropped the squad down on the ground. A barrage of small-arms fire followed. The American squad maneuvered quickly on their stomachs and formed a skirmish line to return fire. James dropped down on one knee and shot the soldier nearest to him. He killed two more before the NCO turned around and saw him.

"You motherfucking—" The sergeant died before he could finish the sentence.

James pulled the bright red bandana from his pocket and tied it around his forehead as the prearranged signal to the NVA troops that he was one of them. A soft sound caught James's attention through the din of gunfire, and he looked in the direction it had come from. A black soldier, the only black assigned to the sergeant's squad, was crawling toward the battalion perimeter. James lowered his CAR-15 and hesitated. He let the weapon hang from its sling and ran to catch up to the man.

"Where in the fuck are you going?" James dropped down on his knees next to the soldier.

"Back to the perimeter to get some help. . . .Man, there's hundreds of fucking gooks out there!" The soldier was afraid, but not terrified.

"Did you see anything?" James's voice was threatening.

"Yeah, man! *Gooks!* Now let go of my fucking arm!" The soldier pulled free from James's grip.

"Good . . . You go back to battalion for help, and I'm going to check and see if we have any wounded."

The black soldier looked at James as if he had flipped his lid. "Fucking fine with me!"

James watched the soldier crawl for another ten meters and then jump to his feet and start running. He should have killed him too, but killing black brothers wasn't why he had joined up with the NVA.

The black soldier ran toward his company's portion of the perimeter, where the guards had been alerted and knew that one of their rifle squads would be coming through from the night ambush. The soldier felt his back muscles tighten as he anticipated the bullets from James's CAR-15. He had seen James kill the sergeant and two more of his squad in cold blood.

"Halt!" The challenge came from a log-roofed fighting bunker on the side of a slight rise in the jungle floor.

"Barker! Second squad! Coming through!" The black soldier didn't slow down his stride and flipped into the closest foxhole he could find. "NVA! *Hundreds of them!*"

An M-60 light machine gun started barking a couple of holes down from the black soldier, and then a claymore detonated a few meters away before the familiar cracking from NVA AK-47s answered them.

The platoon leader slid into Barker's foxhole, followed by his radio operator. "What's out there, Barker?"

"Man, sir . . . you aren't going to fucking believe this shit!" Barker took a deep breath and quickly told the lieutenant what had happened to his squad.

* * *

The land-line telephone rang in Lieutenant Van Pao's office twice before she answered the call. It was the division's intelligence officer. He informed her that he would be visiting her camp in two days, and he wanted to personally interrogate the young American POW who was causing her so much trouble. The division commander wanted to know where the secret sensors were located, and he wanted the information before they started their big push into the A Shau Valley the following week.

She was in a very bad mood when James entered her office wearing NVA pants and shirt.

"How do you like my new belt, Lieutenant?" James grabbed the gold belt buckle with the red star centered in it and tilted the shiny metal fastener for her to see.

"Very nice, soldier." Van Pao didn't look up from the papers on her desk. "I called you here to tell you that a colonel from Division is coming to visit us, and he *hates* Americans. Stay out of his way, and when you meet him, show respect, or he'll kill you on the spot."

"Did he hear about my patrol?" James was smiling.

"Yes—that's why you're still alive." Lieutenant Van Pao had had enough conversation with James. "Now go." She nodded back toward the door. Mohammed James was a great coup for her, and he was gaining a reputation even as high as corps level. What bothered her most was that he could betray his own people and *enjoy* doing it.

"Lieutenant?"

"Yes!"

"Could I take Garibaldi and Barnett down to the river today?"

Lieutenant Van Pao thought for a minute and then decided that it would be a good idea to let Barnett swim in the river and enjoy himself; directly after, she would make her last attempt at breaking him before the division staff officer arrived at her camp. "Yes, take them and some guards; with the Americans so close to us in the A Shau Valley, they might send a patrol over here in neutral Laos."

"I'll have them back early." James pressed his lips together and frowned. He loved taking the other two Americans down to the river to bathe. The experience gave him a sense of power, especially with Garibaldi being a full bird colonel and Barnett hating blacks so much. The games he played with them were mostly brain games and didn't do much harm, but he would get the guards to beat them if they didn't obey him.

A pair of armed NVA soldiers led the way down to the river where a shallow sun-heated pool made a perfect giant bathtub. The soldiers were happy because they enjoyed cooling off in the river as much as the prisoners did. Barnett didn't dare look back, but he knew that James was right behind him. Garibaldi had to help him hobble down the path.

"Let's move it faster!" James made a point out of "accidentally" kicking Barnett's heel.

A muffled scream left the younger soldier's throat. His feet were just beginning to heal and were still extremely sore.

"Something wrong with you, *Spence*?" James used the nickname Woods had found for him back at An Khe base camp.

Barnett continued hobbling. Garibaldi could feel that the young soldier had shifted more of his weight to him. "We're almost there. . . ."

James tripped Garibaldi and sent both of the POWs rolling down the dew-covered embankment. "Who said you could talk, *Colonel*?"

"No one, sir . . . Sorry, sir." Garibaldi had been a POW long enough to know what James was looking for, and he wasn't going to give him any reason to beat him or Barnett.

"You're damn right! Say *sir* again."

"Sir."

"That sounds good. . . . Maybe you'll be able to call me *General* James one of these days. . . . If I kill enough Americans, they just might promote me to a general." This was the first time that James had admitted killing American soldiers to anyone except the NVA.

Garibaldi squeezed Barnett's arm to warn him to keep quiet and not piss James off. Barnett was sharp enough to realize that James had made a very bad error in bragging about killing his fellow GIs, unless James didn't think Garibaldi or he would live to tell anyone about it.

The Rao Lao River appeared through the thick underbrush and gave Garibaldi a chance to change the subject. "Sir?"

"Huh?" Mohammed James glared over at the Air Force fighter pilot.

"Is it all right, sir, for Spencer and me to use the shallow part of the pool first?" Garibaldi lowered his eyes to the ground as he waited for James's answer.

"Why?"

"So Barnett can soak his feet in the cool water under those trees."

"Yeah . . . go ahead."

Colonel Garibaldi helped Spencer over to the shade-cooled water and assisted the soldier. It really didn't matter what temperature the water was, but Garibaldi knew that the NVA guards liked the deeper end of the pool, especially when they came to the giant tub with James, who enjoyed walking around the rocks naked. The shorter NVA soldiers could be waist deep in the water and have some privacy.

Two of the NVA took up positions overlooking the bathers, with angry looks thrown at those who had won the card cutting to determine who would be first in the water.

Garibaldi waited until James had joined the NVA soldiers in the deep end before talking to Spencer. "They're up to something, Spence. The guards were whispering all day today, and every time I drew close to them they would stop talking until I left."

"What do you think is going on?" Spencer was looking down the river. His thoughts were on how close they were to South Vietnam and the A Shau Valley. Their POW camp at A Rum was just a couple of miles over the border. He wondered if Sweet Bitch had beaten his feet so that he couldn't attempt an escape, or if she really still needed the information on the sensors. He knew that he couldn't survive another one of those beatings without telling her anything she wanted to know. In fact, she didn't know just how close she had come to breaking him. If he hadn't passed out from the pain, Spencer knew he would have talked. He glanced over at James and lowered his eyelids. He wanted to kill James more than anything on earth. He had seen him leaving the camp with his CAR-15 a number of times, and he now knew what James was doing for the NVA and why they allowed him to have a private hooch and a woman.

James must have sensed Barnett staring at him and turned around slowly. Barnett reached down beside his legs and splashed water over his chest. James smiled. He was going to enjoy killing Spencer, but he was going to do it very, very slowly.

"Watch out, here he comes. . . ." Garibaldi spoke without moving his lips.

James stopped next to his pile of clothes and removed two cans of olive-drab C-rations and a pair of white plastic spoons. He strolled next to the river naked and stopped twice to kick at the water with his feet. James couldn't swim, but he liked the water. He stopped walking when he reached the pair of POWs and looked down at Spencer from less than a foot away. "I thought you'd like something to eat. . . ." He set the cans of food down on a rock just out of Garibaldi's reach. Spencer could have taken the cans if he wanted to.

"What's the price?" Spencer knew that James hated him too much to just give him something.

Garibaldi read the labels on the cans of fruit. One was peaches; the other, fruit cocktail. The colonel's body craved the fruit and sweet sugared juice.

"No price . . . I'm just being nice." James handed a U.S. Army P-38 opener to Spencer. "We got to start trying to get along a little better . . . and I heard Lieutenant Van Pao tell her sergeant that they were going to put you in Mother Kaa's cage tonight. . . ." James paused, looking for a reaction from Spencer. He got it from the colonel.

"Those bastards!"

"You shut the fuck up, Colonel!" James backhanded the senior officer hard enough to bring blood between his teeth. The short break away from Spencer gave him time to catch his fear and hide it from the traitor.

"So what? I could give a fuck about that snake. . . . I'm too big for the bitch to eat, and if she fucks with me I might eat *her*!" Spencer smiled to hide the fear that was trying to make his upper lip tremble.

"Eat the fruit and maybe you'll smell like something good to eat and she'll try . . . maybe nibbling on your leg. . . ." James hissed. The noise sent a shiver down Spencer's spine.

"In that case, I will. . . ." Spencer opened the first can and started eating the fruit slowly.

James laughed and went back over to where the NVA guards were drying off so that they could relieve their comrades on guard duty.

Spencer waited until James had turned his back and quickly handed the open can of fruit cocktail to the colonel.

"Thanks, Spencer!" Garibaldi was starting to get the first symptoms of scurvy. His teeth were already loose, and his gums would bleed if he just pressed his fingers against them.

Spencer held the can of sliced peaches in his hand and read the label. His mouth started watering in anticipation. He stopped himself from punching a hole in the lid and handed the second can over to the colonel. "Here . . . for later."

"I can't take both of them, Spencer . . . I just can't." Garibaldi shook his head.

"Please . . . I don't think I could stand looking at you if all of your teeth fell out!" Barnett smiled. "Here . . . please take it."

Garibaldi hesitated and took the food that was medicine to him. "Spencer, when we get back to the States, I promise you . . . I'm going to buy you a *case* of Del Monte Fruit Cocktail!"

"It's a deal." Spencer looked over at the guards. "You'd better hide the can; here comes a guard."

The NVA beckoned for the POWs to get dressed for the return trip to the camp.

Lieutenant Van Pao was waiting for them when they returned from the river. She waited until Garibaldi had helped Barnett into his cage and then called him over to where she stood. She was very angry at how badly Barnett had been beaten by James, but she had to assume the responsibility because she had given her permission. It was the last time, though, that she would allow James to touch one of her prisoners.

"Colonel Garibaldi, ma'am."

"Colonel, come with me to my office." She whirled around and walked rapidly back to her office. Garibaldi relaxed when he saw that she entered the building from the side where she worked and not the end of the structure where she did her interrogations.

Van Pao took a seat and opened a cardboard sundries box that was normally issued to American troops. She removed a carton of Marlboro cigarettes and placed one of the packages on her desk. Garibaldi watched the NVA officer light up. He realized at the same time that someone must be supplying the NVA with American supplies, for the popular sundries package to be there. The American troops liked them in the field because the sundries boxes included free cigarettes that were fresh, not like the C-ration cigarettes that were always stale and tasted funny. The packages also contained candy and shaving equipment.

"Would you like a cigarette, Colonel?" Van Pao smiled and offered the pack.

"I don't smoke, ma'am."

"Candy?" She held out a small carton containing twenty-four Chuckles.

"Sure . . ." He took the package and started opening it to remove one of the smaller boxes of the popular red, yellow, green, black, and orange candies.

"Keep them all." She waved back the offered package.

"Thank you." Garibaldi's thoughts flashed back to the

river when Spencer asked James what the price was for the offered food.

"I would like a small favor from you." Lieutenant Van Pao became all business. "Spencer Barnett has some information that I need, and I want him to talk before our division staff sends a certain officer here to interrogate him." She leaned forward and spoke slowly. "This officer is known for his cruel methods of extracting information."

"What would you like to know?" Garibaldi already knew the answer.

"His reconnaissance team hid some secret sensor equipment along the Ho Chi Minh Trail. We have found half of it, and we *will* find the rest . . . it's all just a matter of time. There is an engineer company assigned to that task." Van Pao inhaled a deep breath of smoke and leaned back in her chair. "He can make living here a lot easier on himself if he cooperates. . . . He makes me look good, and I can make *both* of your lives much, much more tolerable here in my camp."

"I'll talk to Barnett." Garibaldi knew that Spencer couldn't take much more torture and that the sensors weren't worth the young man's life. The edge of a Polaroid photograph was sticking out from under the NVA intelligence officer's desk and caught Garibaldi's eye when he looked down. He could see that the man tied to the bamboo rod was Barnett, but he couldn't see who was wielding the bamboo cat-o'-nine-tails. He didn't hesitate; if he had taken the time to think, he wouldn't have done it. The photograph could have been a set-up.

Garibaldi dropped the box of candy to the floor and then fell on all fours to retrieve it. He shoved the photograph into the box and almost gave himself away when he saw that it was James who was beating Spencer. Garibaldi hid his gasp by coughing.

"Barnett has until dark, and then I have something *special* for him that I'm quite sure will be convincing as to my dedication." Lieutenant Van Pao instructed the guard to take the colonel over to Barnett's cage and let him talk to him until dark.

Spencer was set in his decision to hold out as long as he possibly could before revealing what he knew about the sensors. It was obvious that the NVA wanted the devices destroyed, and that could only mean the seismic-intrusion devices were causing them a great deal of trouble. Every day he could hold out meant a day longer that the North Vietnamese were suffering casualties because of him.

"Spence, I know what you're thinking and how you feel, but a night with Mother Kaa... No one will hold it against you if you talk now." Colonel Garibaldi's voice was soft. "Besides, the photograph of James beating you will surely be proof enough as to what you've put up with under torture!"

"No... I might not make it through the night without spilling my guts to those bastards, but I've got to try...." Spencer's eyes were locked on Mother Kaa's cage. She had been sleeping all day long and would probably be very active once the sun dropped behind the mountains.

Colonel Garibaldi respected Barnett's dedication, but he also knew that when the boy broke under torture, he was the type who couldn't be put back together again. "All right, then... I'm not going to waste any more time trying to convince you." The colonel leaned forward and spoke in lower tones. "Let's talk about Mother Kaa.... I don't want to scare you, but if they put you in her cage tonight, you'd better know a few things about large snakes."

"Like what?" Spencer's voice quavered in front of his fellow prisoner.

"Normally, I don't think she would try... eating..." —Garibaldi hesitated for a second with the word and then said it anyway; he had to make it clear to Spencer what he was in for and what he could do to protect himself—"... an adult human, but she's one *big* bitch, and you've lost a lot of weight."

"Do you really think..." Barnett couldn't take his eyes

off the cage. He was imagining a long bump in her body come morning that would be him. "Man! . . . Colonel, I'm scared."

Garibaldi hugged the young soldier. There was really nothing else he could do to try to reassure him. "Listen: You are going to make it out of this fucking place! Think *positive!*"

Spencer's eyes opened wider and wider as he watched the thirty-six-foot-long python slowly move her coils.

"Spence!" Garibaldi's voice was sharp. "Listen to me! I'll be awake all night long with you . . . and this is what I want you to do: First, talk to me, tell me everything that's going on in the cage once it gets dark and I can't see. Second," —Garibaldi didn't want to say it, but he had to warn Spencer—"protect your head. If she's going to try anything, she'll try biting your head and start there. . . . But she *has* to bite you somewhere, in order to get traction with her coils."

Spencer's voice broke, and tears rolled over his cheeks. "Oh . . . shit . . . Colonel . . . I'm so fucking scared!"

"Spence . . . do you want to change your mind? It's all right if you do." Garibaldi grabbed both of Spencer's shoulders and gently shook him to get his attention. "Spencer! You've done far more than most *men.* . . . There's nothing wrong in giving in now!"

Spencer lifted his chin and looked at the colonel. The tears filling his eyes magnified the light blue irises. Garibaldi felt a pain in his chest. He would gladly trade places with the seventeen-year-old. He was in his mid-forties and had lived a good life until he had been shot down; this soldier was barely into puberty and had so much to live for.

Garibaldi hugged the boy tightly in his arms and felt the thin shoulders shaking. "I want you to know, Spencer, that I am very proud of you . . . *very proud.*" The colonel's tears soaked through Spencer's hair. "Your father is one very lucky man to have a son like you."

Spencer wrapped his arms around the colonel and hugged back. "Oh . . . fuck, sir . . . I'm scared."

*   *   *

Lieutenant Van Pao watched the emotional scene from the shadows of her troop barracks. She couldn't make out what was going on—if Spencer had broken down or if he was confiding in the colonel father figure. She left the shadows and approached the cage.

"Spencer . . . would you like to talk to me?"

Barnett released his hold on the colonel and glared at the North Vietnamese intelligence officer. "Fuck you, Sweet Bitch!"

The blunt, hostile statement caught her off guard, and she hesitated with her mouth opening and closing like a fish's out of water. Finally she spoke. "You will see what a Sweet Bitch really is!" She turned and gave the guards orders.

The camp guards pulled Spencer out of the cage along with the colonel. Van Pao backhanded Garibaldi across his mouth, drawing blood instantly. "You failed me!" She turned her attention to Spencer and nodded her head. The guards tore his black pajamas from his body, leaving him naked. "There will not be a repeat of what happened to our South Vietnamese officer. . . . Mother Kaa will not have any problems digesting *you*!"

The guards pulled Barnett to the python's cage and lifted him on top of the structure. The snake was coiled up in a tight ball at one end of the low bamboo cage. Spencer dropped down through the roof hole and scooted to the opposite side of the cage. He felt the cool bamboo poles against his buttocks and knew that he could go no farther back.

"Call me anytime, if you have something to tell me." Lieutenant Van Pao smiled and ran her fingers back and forth along the bamboo bars, making a soft scraping noise. "Wake up . . . Mother Kaa, wake up. . . ."

Garibaldi watched from his cage. He instantly picked up the name Van Pao was calling the snake and realized that there was only one way that she could have known they called the python by that nickname. Garibaldi was positive they had never referred to the snake by that name in front of her, but they did talk openly in front of the guards. Garibaldi was sure that some of the guards spoke English. They only pretended that they couldn't understand what was said to them so that they could eavesdrop on the POWs' conversations.

Spencer stared at the huge pile of coils. She seemed a lot bigger close up than in the failing light. The coils moved slowly and the monster python's head appeared. She looked directly at Spencer with her black, lifeless eyes and tested the air with her tongue.

Lieutenant Van Pao left to have supper with her men. The single remaining guard retired to the small guard shack to smoke a cigarette. The guard knew that he wouldn't be able to sleep once it got dark, with the POW screaming all night long like the South Vietnamese officer had done.

Colonel Garibaldi saw Spencer's chest heaving in and out rapidly and knew the soldier was scared to the point of hyperventilating. "Spence . . . take it easy, boy. She's only a dumb reptile . . . remember that! We'll outsmart her, boy. . . . *Spencer!* Talk to me."

The colonel's voice was a comfort to Barnett, and he quickly gained control of himself. "I'm fine, Colonel."

"Good! Now back up into one of the corners of the cage, and if she starts moving, don't let her get her head behind you and push you away from the bamboo. . . . She can't coil or squeeze you without getting some kind of traction."

"All right." Spencer scooted from his position against the bamboo bars to a corner of the cage. Mother Kaa's head didn't move, but she tested the air again. "Man, Colonel . . . she has a head as big as a football!"

"She might try and coil up against you for warmth when it gets dark. . . . Be ready for that too." Garibaldi looked over at the guard in the shack and wondered if he could speak English.

Spencer pushed his back against the corner of the cage and pulled his knees up to his chest. He wrapped his arms around his legs and waited.

* * *

The old Montagnard sat on his porch with three more of the village elders and sipped the bamboo straw that stuck out of the large wine pot in front of him. A length of bamboo had been placed over the lip of the jug with a splinter of bamboo about two inches long bent down into the jug. The purpose of the stick was to measure how much each man drank. When it was your turn to drink through your straw, water was poured in the jug until it reached the very lip and was going to overflow. You drank through your straw until the level of the wine lowered and the sliver of bamboo was exposed. There was no faking drinking at a Montagnard wine-drinking ceremony. What made it even worse was that they were constantly adding new water to the wine, and since it was drawn up from the bottom of the pot, the wine would actually still be fermenting in your stomach. There wasn't a worse drunk and hangover than the ones created from Montagnard *num-pah*.

As the Bru chieftain saw the sun drop down behind the mountain, his vision disappeared. He was suffering from a severe vitamin-A deficiency and would be totally blind before the year was out. The old man spoke to the other elders and asked that they beg the evil Tang Lie to leave them alone in peace. The other old men began chanting and beating their gongs. The music reached the POW camp and would have provided a refreshing form of entertainment, except for the situation Spencer was in.

The sun dropped even lower in the sky, and the long, dark shadows filled the camp. Garibaldi couldn't make out Spencer's form in the cage, but he kept talking to him. The darkness was making it even more difficult for Spencer.

"She . . . she's starting to move, Colonel." Spencer's voice echoed with fear.

"Take it easy. . . . She's just going to check you out. . . . Remember to keep your back pressed against the cage." Garibaldi didn't know if his advice was any good; the snake was so big and so powerful, she could probably wedge herself between the soldier and the bars without any major effort, but he had to tell the boy something.

"Oh . . . fuck . . . fuck . . . fuck . . ."

"What's wrong?"

"Her head's less than a foot from me! Shit, Colonel . . . I can't take this shit!" Spencer's voice broke.

A scream forming on Spencer's lips bubbled out just as a long narrow bamboo stick appeared through the bottom matting of the cage about two inches in front of the snake's head. A second later, another one of the finger-sized sticks appeared through the floor about five inches away from the first. Mother Kaa stopped crawling forward and tested the flimsy barrier with her tongue. The hot peppers that the sticks had been soaked in instantly burned her sense organs, and her head jerked back. The sticks kept appearing through the floor until a wall had been created around Spencer from the floor to the roof. Spencer blinked his eyes to see if the newly created wall was real or just part of his imagination. The bamboo was real.

The Bru chieftain's grandson had been hiding under the snake's cage all afternoon. His grandfather had overheard the Vietnamese talking about putting the small American in with the snake, and the chief had devised this plan with the stakes and Montagnard antisnake potion. The boy lay on his back and listened to his grandfather chant him directions from the porch of his longhouse. The gongs reassured the small boy that Ae Die, their village god, would bring him much happiness for the brave deed he was doing for the American. The Bru ceremony would last all night long, and the boy knew he would have to remain awake to remove the sticks when his grandfather and the other elders warned him that the Vietnamese were coming to check up on the prisoner.

Garibaldi listened to the Montagnard music and the singing that was so basic and yet somehow so reassuring. He hadn't heard a word from Spencer since it had gotten dark and called softly over to him. "Spence? You OK?"

"Sir, you won't believe it. . . ." Spencer's voice was filled with his old self-confidence.

"What?"

"I'll tell you in the morning. . . . Right now I want to get some rest." Spencer rested his chin against his legs and closed his eyes.

CHAPTER FOUR

Da Nang

Private First Class—soon to be Specialist Fourth Class—David Woods left the back of the truck and waved his thanks to the driver. He had hitchhiked from the First Cavalry base camp at An Khe to the naval hospital in Da Nang to see his teammate Reggie Sinclair. Lieutenant Reed had given Woods a three-day in-country leave to make the trip after their successful mission in the A Shau to retrieve the seismic-intrusion detectors.

"Be waiting out in front of the hospital by noon!" Sergeant Shaw called back to where Woods was standing. "I ain't going to wait for you and end up having to drive back down to An Khe in the dark!"

"I'll be here! Thanks, Sarge!" Woods left the roadside and entered the hospital compound through the main gate. Dual machine gun bunkers guarded the entrance in a symbolic gesture for security. The hospital was protected from attack by the large red crosses painted on each of the buildings and the fact that North Vietnamese and Vietcong prisoners of war were treated there exactly the same as an American would be. The idea was great for the humanitarians back in the States, but it lost its appeal to a young Marine or soldier who lost his legs and would wake up from surgery to find an NVA soldier in the bed next to him. It didn't happen very often, but it had happened and had caused a lot of trouble when the Marine tried crawling out of his bed to choke the NVA to death.

Woods checked with the information desk to find out which ward Sinclair was in. He followed the arrows around the quadrangle and then through a maze of wards until he admitted that he was lost. He stopped a friendly-looking nurse and asked for new directions. She showed him the hallway he needed to take and left him with a warm smile.

The sound of the heavy engines from a CH-47 Chinook helicopter drew Woods to a side entrance of the hospital. There were nurses and green-clothed doctors running back and forth along the narrow corridor David was walking down, and he felt that he was getting in their way. A small screen door exited off the narrow hall, and Woods pushed it open and stepped outside to wait until the rush of corpsmen and stretcher bearers had passed.

Woods turned around under the tin-roofed veranda and stood in mute shock at the sight before him. The end of the veranda opposite from where he stood had a large set of double doors that opened out onto the medical helipad. The CH-47 filled the pad, with the rear entrance to the craft facing toward the doors. The steel bed of the chopper was piled with the bodies of dead and dying Marines. Navy corpsmen were pulling the bodies to the edge of the chopper and then lifting them onto stretchers, where a doctor pointed which way to take them—to the morgue or into the veranda, where a crew of corpsmen waited with sharp knives and scissors to cut the web gear and clothes off the wounded. David watched the medical teamwork, not realizing that he was standing openmouthed. It was obvious from the way that the dead and wounded had been packed into the single CH-47 that there hadn't been much time to load them, and that helicopters weren't getting through to where the wounded and dead were—and that the battle was still raging. One of the corpsmen yelled for David to help, and he automatically ran over to the chopper and scrambled on board. He could feel his traction-soled jungle boots slip on the blood-covered steel floor, and he fell to his knees. David's face was inches away from the open eyes of a dead leatherneck.

"Man . . . help me . . ." The voice of a wounded Marine drew David's attention away from the dead. He shoved the open-eyed Marine over to one side and tugged gently at the wounded man. A low groan came from the Marine, and David stopped pulling, thinking that he was hurting him.

"Don't stop now . . . get me the fuck out of this meat wagon!" The Marine tried smiling, but his slashed upper lip hung from his nose by a small fragment of skin.

Woods lifted the man onto a stretcher, and two corpsmen carried him back under the veranda. David stepped back away from the chopper and let the white-suited corpsmen finish. He wondered why the medics wore white; it only made the bright red blood show up better. Woods's eyes locked onto a corner of the helicopter's lowered tailgate where a stream of blood oozed between the cracks where the gate hinged to the body of the chopper. He didn't know what made him look down, but he did. A single human finger lay on the sand in a pool of collective blood from the Marines. David didn't have a problem knowing which finger on a human hand it was, because there was a high school graduation ring still attached to it.

David blinked and told his mind to think of nothing, absolutely nothing. It was his personal way of maintaining his sanity. He had learned to do that when his dog had been killed by a car when he was seven years old, and it had always worked for him ever since.

The veranda was packed with medical personnel. At first glance, it looked as if no one knew what he was doing, but it was a perfectly functioning team. A two-inch water pipe had been installed around the veranda by the Navy Seabees, and every two feet there was a faucet with a twenty-five-foot garden-sized hose attached to it. A corpsman used the hose to wash down the naked bodies of the wounded. The process seemed barbaric and backward for medical techniques in the sixties, but it was the fastest way to wash the mud and filth from the wounded so that surgeons and nurses could evaluate the wounds.

Woods felt his back dig into the screen and wood wall. He watched the pink water flow to the drains and swirl in the opposite direction of the earth's rotation down into the ground underneath South Vietnam.

"Soldier! What are you doing in here?" A white-haired nurse paused in her tasks and frowned up at Woods. "This is off limits to you!"

"Sorry, ma'am . . ." David felt behind him for the door and stumbled through it. He walked down the hallway until he reached an intersection and stopped; he could feel a cool breeze coming off the South China Sea against his wet face and realized that he had been sweating profusely. His jacket and the top four inches of his waistband were saturated.

A nurse standing behind a counter looked up and saw the look on the young soldier's face and knew instantly that he was in some sort of shock. She left the desk and approached him slowly. "Can I help you, soldier?" Her voice was soothing, and David's head turned toward her, but his eyes still weren't focusing; it was as if he were blind.

"He stumbled into the post-op receiving area. . . . We've just received a load of wounded coming in from a big battle up at Khe Sanh. It was the first aircraft that could get in there in the last three days of fighting. . . . It was a mess." A corpsman wearing a blood-splattered apron stood behind Woods and explained what had happened.

"Thanks, Corpsman. . . . I'll take care of him." The nurse put her arm over Woods's shoulder and guided him down the hall. "Come on . . . I'll buy you a cup of coffee."

The open-air veranda of the hospital that faced the sea was filled with doctors and nurses on break. A small cafeteria operated out of one corner. The nurse carried two cups of black coffee to the table where David sat and waited.

"Here . . ." She set a cup down in front of him.

"Thanks." He was regrouping his emotions and spoke in a clipped voice.

"War *is* hell." Her voice was soft. She wasn't mocking the soldier.

"I know." Woods tilted his head to one side and grinned.

"And your name is?"

"David Woods."

"David . . . beloved of God . . . I think that is the correct English interpretation for it." She sipped from her hot cup.

"And you?"

"Natasha MacReal . . . nurse . . . one week in-country . . . and ready to leave!" She nodded her head as if to accent the last word.

"Thanks."

"Oh, it's nothing. . . . The post-op receiving area by the helipad is *not* the place to be when they bring in the wounded. You were very unlucky to have stumbled in there. . . ." She smiled. "If it will help, I've seen doctors lose their breakfasts the first time they worked it."

"It wasn't seeing the wounded. . . ." David looked down inside of his coffee cup and couldn't see the bottom. He knew that he couldn't because of the dark coffee filling the Styrofoam cup, but he got angry because he *wanted* to; he wanted to *control* something that he knew he couldn't. He thought of the single finger lying in the bloody sand and wondered what high school the Marine had gone to. "I should have looked." His voice was a raspy whisper.

"Looked at what?" Natasha offered a puzzled smile.

"Oh . . . nothing . . . something personal." Woods pushed the wicker chair back and stood up. "Hey! It was nice talking to you, but I've got to find my buddy before they come to get me."

"Is he here in the hospital?"

"Yes . . . Reggie Sinclair."

"Reggie!" Natasha clapped her hands. "He's the one who's trying to ship two Eurasian kids back home!"

"Yeah. Do you know which ward he's in?"

"Sure! C'mon . . ." She led the way across the open-air patio to a doorway. "I think everyone here is in love with those kids."

David Woods looked up at the hot sun without blinking
and sighed so deeply that his soul quivered. He was hurting
inside; he felt like he was changing into something he knew
he wouldn't like when the process was done. He mumbled
under his breath the thought that flashed into his mind as he
followed the nurse: "I should have *looked*. . . ." Instantly his
rational mind reacted to the morbid thought, and he added,
"You sick fucking bastard."

Natasha turned her head slightly and looked back at
Woods out of the corner of her eye.

Sinclair was sitting up in his bed when Woods entered the
ward. Little Jean-Paul and Trung were helping the duty
nurse with some of her chores. An Army colonel wearing
clean, pressed short-sleeved khakis sat on the edge of Sinclair's bed.

Sinclair looked up and saw his teammate. "David! Come
here and meet my dad." Reggie waved for him to hurry
over.

Trung looked up from the magazines she was stacking and
ran to fling herself into Woods's arms.

"Whoa! You're getting *fat* eating hamburgers and french
fries." David laughed and sat the tiny girl back down on the
floor. He took a second to recall how frail she had looked
just a few weeks earlier. Even her older brother, Jean-Paul,
had put on a little weight and looked healthier. The hospital
staff was spoiling them. A person would never have suspected that just a few days earlier both of the Eurasian kids
had been living off garbage and what they could beg on the
streets. A lot of love and good food had made a big difference. Woods suspected it was the love that had helped the
most.

Reggie's voice broke into David's thought. "Dad, this is
David Woods. He's the guy I told you about who saved my
ass on patrol."

The Army colonel held out his hand. "It's a real pleasure
meeting you. My wife and I want to thank you for saving
our son's life."

Woods smiled and shook his head from side to side. "Is that what he's told you?"

"Come off it, David!" Sinclair tried reaching over and cuffing his friend, but Woods leaned back out of range.

"He sure did!" As the colonel looked over at his son, love for the young soldier radiated out of his eyes. "Reggie told me that you carried him under fire to the helicopter when you could have just left him and saved yourself."

The colonel had no way of knowing the impact of what he had said. The last five words in his sentence cut through Woods like a laser. David's face turned white. Reggie saw what was happening and moved over to where he could reach up and touch his friend.

"Dave . . . Dad doesn't know about . . . Spence." Reggie's voice was apologetic.

"About who?" The colonel could see that he had touched a sore spot.

Woods blinked back his emotion and looked directly into the colonel's eyes. "Spencer Barnett was part of our team. When we got ambushed, he stayed back as a rear guard . . ." Woods turned his head away from the officer and continued.

"Spence told me to get on the chopper and help Reggie. I-left-him-there-and-he-got-captured-by-the-NVA." The only way the last sentence could come out of him was rapidfire, like a verbal machine gun.

"Oh . . . now I think I understand." Colonel Sinclair could see the guilt written on Woods's face. "Let's go over it again, but this time *in detail*."

Reggie looked at his father as if the colonel had gone nuts. The older man gave his son a trust-me-I-know-what-I'm-doing look. Reggie sighed and leaned back against his double pillows.

"I don't think I want to do that . . . sir." Woods shook his head and bit his bottom lip gently. "Thanks anyway . . ."

"Nurse?" Colonel Sinclair beckoned to the duty nurse. "Would you lend me one of your clipboards and some paper?"

The nurse sent Jean-Paul over with the requested items. A lead pencil was shoved under the clip.

"All right, David. Draw me a picture of the ambush site." The colonel held out the clipboard. Woods hesitated for a long time, but the colonel kept the clipboard in front of him; slowly, Woods took it and began drawing. He felt the colonel's arm slip over his shoulder, and a reassuring squeeze told him that it would be all right. Woods started drawing faster.

"Now . . . put in everyone's position. . . ."

David marked the spots on the map where he last saw each of the team members, including Fitzpatrick and the two Special Forces sergeants who had been hit by the Chinese claymore mine.

"Fine . . . Now let's go through it again, but this time show me on the map as you talk."

Reggie could see that Woods was getting into the briefing, and each time Woods would balk, his father would gently prompt him with a comment about the tactics of the recon team's withdrawal.

Woods finished and dropped the clipboard and pencil down on the hospital sheet.

"So, David! Why all the guilt?" The blunt statement from the colonel shattered the soldier's last defensive barrier.

David Woods started crying hard. "Because I promised Spence that I wouldn't leave him if he was alive. . . . We had made a deal that we wouldn't leave each other on a battle-field alive so the NVA could capture us. . . . We promised each other that we would put a bullet through our heads rather than allow the NVA to fuck with us. And I *left Spence*! I broke my promise!"

"Hold it!" Colonel Sinclair's voice cut through Woods's self-pity. "Was Barnett wounded?"

Woods shook his head.

"He wasn't wounded? OK . . . What was he doing?"

"He was the rear guard when Reg got hit." The words came out between sobs.

"David! Stop feeling guilty!" The colonel stood and adjusted his gigline. "From what you've shown me and from my own personal experiences as a Ranger during Korea, you guys performed a withdrawal from a well-executed ambush ... *perfectly*. Your sergeant should be congratulated for training you so well. As far as leaving Barnett behind goes ... that's bullshit!" Colonel Sinclair tapped Woods's chest hard with his finger. "Bullshit! Do you hear? You could have been the rear guard just as easily, and I would be talking to *Barnett* now instead of you. I'll tell you what!" He took a deep breath. "I took a leave from the Pentagon to come over here and get the paperwork pushed through to bring Trung and Jean-Paul back to our home in the States. That has been taken care of, and I still have a couple of days left." The colonel paused and touched his chin with his fingers in thought before continuing. "I know the staff officer down in Saigon who's in charge of POW recovery. Let me call him on a secure voice radio and find out what they know about Spencer Barnett, and then we can go from there! How about that? Is that fair enough?"

Woods's eyes lit up. "Would you do that?"

"Sure!" The colonel grinned. "But only if you promise me that you'll dump the guilt trip."

Woods nodded his head in agreement. He could feel the guilt lifting from his heart. "One thing, sir."

"Name it."

"If your friend knows where Spence is ... I want to be a member of the team that goes in after him."

Colonel Sinclair stared at Woods for a long time before answering. "Consider it done."

"Thanks, sir."

"*Now*, I've got to go!" What Colonel Sinclair did next caught Woods by surprise. The senior Army officer leaned over and hugged his son and then kissed the soldier on his mouth. "Love you, son."

"Love you too, Dad." There was no embarrassment in Reggie's voice.

Colonel Sinclair stopped on his way out and picked up each of the children in his arms and repeated the hug and kiss. The other occupants of the ward watched the emotional farewell.

"You've got one hell of a good dad there. . . ." Woods nodded his head.

"I know." Reggie Sinclair smiled proudly as his father left the ward.

Sergeant Shaw pulled the canvas cover over the cases of supplies they had loaded up at the Da Nang depot. He had the two-and-a-half-ton truck loaded all the way to the rear tailgate with boxes of hard-to-get items.

"Simpson! Stay with the truck while I run inside and get the paperwork!" Shaw hiked up his jungle fatigues and hopped up the three wooden steps to the depot office. He was in a good mood, despite the heat.

A staff sergeant major sat behind a Plexiglas wall in a corner of the long office building, smoking a cigar. Shaw entered the office without knocking and felt the cool blast from the air conditioner operating at its highest level. "It's pretty damn hot out there!"

The senior sergeant ignored the comment. "Well! Are you satisfied?"

"Almost . . . I sure would like to get a dozen or so of those new CAR-15s. . . ."

"So would everyone else in Vietnam."

"Keep me in mind."

"I will." The sergeant major tapped the edge of his cigar against his desk over a wastepaper basket. "Ahh-hem . . . Do you have something for me?"

Shaw reached down in his side pocket and removed a thick brown manila envelope. He tossed the package on the desk. The senior NCO tore open a corner and peeked inside before pulling open the top drawer of his desk and tossing it in.

"Aren't you going to count it?"

"I *trust* you." He inhaled a deep lungful of blue smoke and blew it toward the air conditioner. "When are you returning for another load?"

"I don't know . . . maybe a month."

"I rotate back to the States in three weeks, but there'll be someone here to take care of you."

"Why are you going back?"

"The colonel is *forcing* me to rotate. I think he's getting a little suspicious, but it's about time I get back home and check up on some things. My new house is about done in Petersburg, and my wife says it'll take two hundred thousand to furnish it. . . ." The sergeant major shook his head. "Fucking woman spends money like I've got a footlocker full of it."

Shaw raised his eyebrows and smiled.

The senior sergeant laughed and slapped the top of his desk. "If she only knew!"

"What have you told her?"

"*Poker* winnings!" He chuckled. "You know I'm lucky at cards!"

"Yeah . . . me too."

Shaw left the office and hurried over to the truck. Simpson was waiting for him, leaning against the shady side of the vehicle and smoking a machine-rolled marijuana cigarette.

"I told you not to smoke that shit while we're working!" Shaw was mad at the black soldier.

"*You're* working, Sarge. . . ." Simpson opened the door to the passenger seat. "When we stop in An Khe, *I'll* go to work."

"I don't know if we'll have time to make a stop." Shaw started the engine. He didn't trust Simpson to drive when the truck was loaded with his personal supplies.

"You make time, Sarge."

"We'll see."

"We'll see shit!" Simpson clenched his teeth. "I helped you, you help me now, or one of us is going to get fucking fragged!"

"Stop the bullshit, Simpson. I'm just fucking with you." Shaw slowed the truck down at the gate and handed the supply depot guard his paperwork. The guard casually checked the manifest and looked at the covered supplies. He gave the sergeant a knowing look and handed the papers back to him.

Shaw shifted gears and pulled out onto Highway 1. "If that fucking Woods isn't waiting out in front of the hospital, we're leaving him! I ain't driving back down to An Khe in the fucking dark, and I don't give a fuck what they say about the road being secured!"

Woods sat next to the machine gun bunker at the main entrance to the naval hospital and smoked a Kool. He felt good for the first time since the ambush. Colonel Sinclair had made a lot of sense; it wasn't a matter of guilt, but of what they could do to get Spence back from the NVA POW camp. He felt sorry for Reggie because he had lost a lung from the bullet wound and then had to stay in the Special Forces camp three days waiting for the weather to clear, but at least Reggie was alive and he didn't smoke, so one lung would last him for the rest of his life. Reggie had told him that they were going to try to ship him home at the same time as they shipped the kids back. David smiled. The two Eurasian kids would find a good home with the Sinclairs. Reggie was half Korean and so were his sisters. Jean-Paul and Trung would fit right in with their family.

Shaw honked the truck horn. Woods grabbed his CAR-15 and ran across the highway to where the truck idled. "You're late."

"Get in!" Shaw nodded for Woods to take a seat on top of the supplies.

David laid his CAR-15 on the canvas and then pulled himself up. A corner of the canvas flipped up, and he could see the pallet of sundry supplies. "Hey, Sarge . . . where did you find the sundries?"

"Pull that canvas down!" Shaw was angry. "You didn't see shit! You hear?"

"Sure, Sarge." Woods realized the sundries weren't for the battalion, but had been bought by Shaw to black-market. A helicopter passed by, flying low to the ground. Woods had no way of knowing that Master Sergeant McDonald was on board heading to the Command and Control North compound located next to Marble Mountain. Woods looked up at the chopper and saw the skull wearing a Green Beret painted on the nose of the aircraft and wondered what Special Forces unit the chopper belonged to. A puff of black diesel smoke made David turn his head away and slide over to the opposite side of the truck. Shaw shifted gears, and the overloaded vehicle pulled away from the side of the road.

Simpson turned around on his seat and called back to Woods, "How's Sinclair doing?"

"Great! He's being shipped back to the States this week, and they're going to try and ship Jean-Paul and Trung back at the same time." Woods adjusted his CAR-15 in his lap so that the charging handle was off his thigh.

"Is he still fucking around with those half-breeds?" Shaw yelled over his shoulder, keeping his eyes on the road.

Woods paused before answering the sergeant. Shaw was an easy man to hate. "*Colonel* Sinclair flew in from the Pentagon to pull some strings for the kids—"

"Sinclair's father is a colonel?" Simpson interrupted.

"A full bird colonel." Woods smiled, knowing Shaw wouldn't like that at all. "He was at the hospital."

"Why would a colonel want to fuck with some Vietnamese street kids?" Shaw still couldn't understand Sinclair's motivation—and considering what made Shaw tick, he probably never would.

"Reggie's an Amerasian. . . ." Woods twisted sideways to light a cigarette.

"A *what*!" Shaw shifted gears and had to yell to be heard over the engine noise.

"Man! *I* know what an Amerasian is!" Simpson felt smart, and the marijuana cigarette he had just finished made him feel talkative. "That's half Vietnamese and half American."

"I still don't know why a *colonel* would want to have two lice-ridden, snot-nosed brats living with him back in the States. . . . Unless he needs a houseboy to shine his shoes."

Shaw smiled, having figured out why the colonel would take the kids back to the States with him.

"I doubt that. . . . Do you know how Vietnamese treat half-breeds, Sergeant?" Woods didn't give the NCO a chance to answer. "They can't attend school, own land, or hold jobs that full-blooded Vietnamese want. They're considered the unwanted offspring of the defeated French. There are even cases where Vietnamese mothers have abandoned their Eurasian offspring so that they wouldn't be associated with having had sex with a Frenchman." Woods looked at the back of Shaw's head and added, "About the only job a Eurasian girl can get is as a whore."

"What's wrong with that?" Shaw looked at the windshield. "Those are some beautiful women!"

Woods agreed that Eurasians were often beautiful people; they seemed to have taken the best features from both races. "Would you want *your* daughter to be a whore?" Woods couldn't resist making the comment.

Shaw turned around on his seat and pointed back at Woods. He held the steering wheel in one hand. "You watch your fucking mouth!"

"I thought so . . ." Woods took a deep lungful of smoke and smiled at the corrupt sergeant.

"Watch the fucking road!" Simpson grabbed for the wheel as the truck veered off onto the shoulder of the road and a red cloud of dust billowed up behind them that covered the windshield of the truck following them.

Woods leaned back against the railing and relaxed for the long drive back to An Khe. He was feeling better than he had felt in months. The talk with Colonel Sinclair had taken a burden off his shoulders that had been destroying him.

Simpson sat thinking on the passenger seat. The THC from the marijuana cigarette had mellowed him out. He reached into his pants pocket and removed a bundle of MPC ten-dollar notes, counted out two hundred of them, and replaced the thick rubber band around the rest. He turned around on the seat and handed the money to Woods. "Here, make out a money order and send this to those kids. Tell the colonel to buy them something nice and let them know that it's from Tousaint Simpson. . . ." He thought for a second and added, "Have him ask them if they still remember me from An Khe."

Woods took the money. "Thanks! I'll do that!"

Shaw looked over at Simpson with an expression on his face that said the soldier had just thrown two thousand dollars out of the truck.

Colonel Sinclair left the hospital and drove back to the XXIV Corps Headquarters where he was staying while he was in Da Nang. He was sharing a room with one of his classmates.

The colonel spoke to the driver. "Drop me off in front of my BOQ and you can turn the jeep in to the motor pool. . . . Thanks." The soldier nodded his head and smiled. He had a trip ticket that was good for the rest of the day and he was going to use it. A steambath and a couple of cold Ba-Moui-Ba beers would hit the spot.

Colonel Sinclair hurried over the cement sidewalk to the building, saluting a group of NCOs on the way. He entered through the rear door and nearly knocked his roommate down.

"What's the rush, Reggie?"

"Sorry, Clyde. . . . I want to change jackets and find a secure voice radio. Do you know where I could use one?"

"Sure . . . We've got a couple secure radios in the G-3 shop. . . . Who do you want to call?"

"I need to talk to Jack Seacourt back at Pentagon East."

"*Brigadier General* Jack Seacourt?"

"Yes . . . he's been given the mission for POW recovery, and I need to talk to him."

"I can do one better for you." The lieutenant colonel nodded his head toward the door. "Let's go over to my shop; I have a direct secure voice land line to the J-3 in Saigon."

"That's great, Clyde!" Sinclair pulled on his clean jacket and followed his classmate out of the building. The sidewalk was lined with banana plants and allowed for the officers to walk in the shade to the large, two-story Corps Headquarters building. The entire structure was made out of wood, screening, and cement-covered sandbags.

Colonel Sinclair took a seat in the private office and placed his call to Brigadier General Seacourt. The general was the highest-ranking member of his graduating class and had been promoted below his promotion zone ever since he had been a second lieutenant. Sinclair had done extremely well and had received numerous accelerated promotions also, but Seacourt was the master politician.

The land line crackled with a little static, and then Seacourt's voice filled the wire. "Reggie! It's good hearing from you again!"

"Hi, Jack. Congratulations on your assignment."

"Well, I don't know if congratulations or a sympathy card is in order. You know, we've never had a successful POW snatch, and there is a lot of pressure on this particular program right now."

Sinclair smiled to himself. He knew that Seacourt had too much political savvy to take on an assignment that would end up making him look bad, especially a combat one. "Well, I'm sure you'll be able to work something out."

"Say, Reggie . . . I left an important meeting to take your call. Is there something I can do for you?" Seacourt waved his hand at the captain, who was signaling him that his staff was waiting.

"Yes, Jack. I need some information on a missing soldier who we think has been captured by the NVA in the A Shau Valley."

Seacourt adjusted the receiver he was holding in his hand against his ear and became very interested. "You say he was captured in the A Shau?"

"Yes . . . about a month ago. . . . His name is—"

"Spencer Barnett."

Sinclair was shocked that the general knew the name of the soldier.

"Or is it Mohammed James?" Seacourt's voice dropped in question.

"No, it's Barnett." Sinclair became very cautious. "He was one of my son's teammates in the First Cavalry Division."

"How's Reggie Junior doing?"

"Fine. He lost a lung and is going home to be discharged."

"Sorry to hear that . . ."

"He's alive, Jack; my wife and I are thankful for that."

"So! What do you want to know about Barnett?"

"Well, has he been taken prisoner, and is he still alive?" Colonel Sinclair looked over at his classmate, who was trying to act busy, but was very interested in the conversation. "And are you going to try and form a snatch team?"

"You know, Reggie, this is a very interesting telephone call. I know you work for the chief of staff back at the Pentagon, but Barnett and James are *very* hot items right now in-country."

"We're on a secure line, Jack, and I have a clearance that is about as high as you can get. . . ." Sinclair left the sentence open.

"Oh! I'm not worried about that, Reggie!" There was a pause and then Seacourt sighed over the line. "Shit! Let me brief you quickly on it. My staff can wait a few minutes." Seacourt's voice settled in for the story. "Last week a young Montagnard boy—about ten years old, maybe younger—came out of Laos to the Special Forces camp at A Shau. He demanded to see the American camp commander and presented the captain with a Polaroid snapshot of Barnett and James."

"A photograph? Were they alive?"

The general paused and then spoke in a very low tone. "Yes, they were alive. Barnett was tied to a bamboo pole and James was whipping him with a bamboo rod. . . . At first we thought the photo was an NVA-staged shot, but experts have blown the photo up, and you can see the actual pain on Barnett's face and . . ." The general paused to swallow. "And the . . . expression of sheer enjoyment on James's face."

"Enjoyment?"

"I've had a lot of experts look at the photograph, and *all* of them agree that James would have to be one hell of a good actor along with Barnett to pose a picture like that. We had the portion where Barnett's feet were exposed—actually, we could only blow up a portion of his left heel up to the ball of his foot, but it was enough to see that Barnett's feet had been severely beaten."

"How did the Montagnard boy get the photograph?"

"This is *very* secret, Reggie...I don't even know if I should say it over this secure telephone...but...the boy said an American gave it to his grandfather and asked if he would deliver it to the Americans at A Shau. From the boy's description, we think the American was an Air Force colonel who was shot down quite a while ago."

"Are you planning a mission?" Sinclair was getting excited.

"Yes. We think they're being held near the Laotian village of A Rum, about three miles inside of Laos." Seacourt nodded again at the captain, who stood impatiently waiting. Sinclair had no way of knowing the meeting concerned exactly what they were now talking about on the telephone. "I've got to run, Reggie. My staff's been waiting for me."

"Just one more thing, Jack...A *big* favor."

"Sure. Ask it."

"There's a young soldier in the First Cavalry who was with Barnett when he was captured. It's very important that he gets on the mission team."

"I'll see what I can do. What's his name?" Seacourt picked up a pencil.

"Specialist Fourth Class David Woods. He's with the First Brigade's Recon Company."

"David Woods...got it. I'll have him involved with the rescue operation in some way. I understand what's going on....I may be a politician, but I still understand troops."

"Thanks, Jack. I owe you one." Sinclair hung up the telephone and felt good about his day's work. He knew that he couldn't mention the telephone conversation to Woods because it was highly classified, but if he knew Seacourt,

Woods would be picked up before sundown and be briefed even better than Sinclair himself had been as to the extent of the mission.

Master Sergeant McDonald sat on the nylon mesh seat in the CCN helicopter and watched the trucks on Highway 1 passing the PSP helipad they were landing on. He did a double take when a heavily loaded deuce-and-a-half's front tires went off the asphalt onto the dirt shoulder, sending up a cloud of red clay dust. He swore that the man riding on top of the load was carrying a CAR-15 submachine gun. The chopper's struts scraped the steel planking, and the rotor blade changed pitch as the aircraft shut down.

A black jeep with the Command and Control North unofficial crest painted under the windshield pulled up and stopped. The driver rested his arms on the top of the wheel and waited for the sergeant to unload. He was the only occupant on the chopper. McDonald dropped his bag on the rear seat and slid his leg over the passenger seat. He could feel the heat coming off the canvas. The jeep had been sitting out in the hot sun, and the seat was hot enough to be very uncomfortable.

"I'll walk. Drop my gear off in the BEQ by the club." McDonald didn't wait for the NCO driver to comment. He was in no mood to be fucked with, and the Green Beret sergeant sensed it.

"There's a piece of cardboard in the back you can sit on." The sergeant tried making up for the crude trick they played on Saigon and Nha Trang staff personnel. The jeep had been left out in the sun intentionally. Most of the staffers would suffer sitting on the hot seat rather than comment to the combat reconnaissance men that the jeep seat was too hot. McDonald had called his bluff.

"I *said* that I'll walk."

The NCO knew he would be laughed out of the club if the master sergeant walked to the Tactical Operations Center. "Sorry, but this is a top-secret area. You have to be escorted."

"I have a TS, *Special Intelligence* clearance, with a 'need-to-know' about everything going on here at CCN. I'll walk where I damn well please.... You can join me if you like." McDonald knew the layout of the compound better than the new NCO driver. He started walking down the sand road.

The sergeant slapped his steering wheel and then pulled the jeep over to the side of the road before running to catch up to McDonald. He could always tell his buddies that the jeep had broken down.

The CCN commander and his deputy watched through the Plexiglas window of his office. They saw McDonald cutting across the sand compound with the NCO running to catch up.

"Didn't anyone tell him about Mac?" The lieutenant colonel addressed his major.

"I guess not!" The major started laughing. "Dumb shit! I can't believe he tried that hot-seat shit on Mac!"

"Get McDonald over to the mission prep area as soon as you brief him." The lieutenant colonel left his office through the back door and walked swiftly on the cement sidewalk to the TOC.

McDonald's mind was filled with a lot of memories as he walked down the familiar sidewalks. A few new buildings had been erected in the compound, but the basic layout was the same. He looked over and saw the row of 100-kw generators that old Felix had scrounged up from the Navy Seabee detachment for a few NVA souvenirs and a couple of trucks. The Seabees had been transferred to Quang Tri and couldn't take the huge electric-making machines with them. McDonald passed the corner of a building and could look back at the row of small hooches where the recon teams were housed, and a flood of mixed memories rushed through him. He stopped walking and the NCO caught up to him.

"Are the Snake Teams still down by the sea?" McDonald didn't look at the sergeant when he asked the question. He kept his eyes glued on the row of buildings and remembered.

The NCO realized that the master sergeant knew too much about CCN to be a staffer. "Sorry about the hot seat, Sarge."

"I didn't like it when they pulled that shit when I was assigned here, and I like it even less now." The look McDonald gave the NCO would keep the man humble for months.

McDonald looked at the camp for a couple of minutes more without saying anything and then abruptly strode off toward the cement TOC.

The major was waiting inside the air-conditioned building and smiled when McDonald entered through the heavy steel door. "Good seeing you again, Mac!"

The NCO escorting the master sergeant felt like hiding in a hole. It was obvious that the NCO Master Sergeant was well known at CCN.

"What happened to your jeep?" The major addressed McDonald.

"It broke down as soon as we started leaving the main gate. You'd better check your mechanics out for VC. . . . It looks like a case of sabotage to me!" McDonald smiled.

"We've been having a lot of mechanical problems lately in camp." The major went along with the master sergeant. "Let's go in the back room and I'll brief you on what we already know."

McDonald nodded his head and followed the major.

When they were gone, the NCO escort turned and spoke to one of the Area Studies team NCOs. "Who the fuck is he?"

The sergeant looked up from the AO map he was posting with information. "You don't know McDonald? Shit . . . he's a legend in his own time. He's only the *best* Project Cherry man CCN ever had—or will have, for that matter."

The escort sergeant's face turned white, and a soft sigh slipped out from between his lips. He had fucked up big-time, and when the story got out he'd be teased until the day he left CCN.

The major took a seat next to McDonald in front of the large briefing map and turned down the room lights so that the map lights would stand out. The briefing was short and to the point. A message had come from Saigon that confirmed a POW camp near the village of A Rum in Laos, and satellite photographs confirmed the village had grown considerably during the past six months. The NVA had camouflaged the area well, but the intelligence people had figured out where the POWs were being held, down to a ten-meter guess.

"The boss wants to show you something over in the isolation area; it's too hot to be discussed even in here." The major was impressed; even he hadn't been briefed on what the lieutenant colonel was going to tell McDonald.

"Fine. When?" McDonald felt very tired and wanted a few minutes alone.

"Right now."

"Let's go and get it over with. I'm tired."

The isolation area was set aside from the rest of the buildings and surrounded by a solid wooden fence so that no one could see in or out. A team would be sent into the isolation area a couple of days before its members were inserted in their operations area, and during that time they weren't allowed to talk with anyone outside of their own Area Studies Team and senior officers. Everyone entering and leaving the isolation area was searched, with their name and purpose for being there logged in. The whole procedure had been established to protect the teams from double agents and informers. CCN had gone through a really bad period when they had lost seventy percent of their teams after they had been inserted in their AOs, and that didn't include all of the helicopters and fixed-wing aircraft lost in support. The NVA spy network was uncovered after a great deal of difficulty, and CCN had been shut down for three months. All of the double agents and supporters of the spy network were found in a thousand-meter area of North Vietnam. In their escape attempt from South Vietnam, none of their parachutes had opened.

McDonald took a deep breath before stepping through the

gate and leaned against the wooden wall that had been erected for that purpose. He was searched and everything was emptied from his pockets and placed into a large manila envelope that would be held for him until he left the high-security area. The hallway and rooms were painfully familiar, and McDonald felt an old fear returning, in the form of a claustrophobic reaction. He had never entered the isolation building without leaving directly from it on a mission. This would be his first time to enter the building and walk back out the front door.

The lieutenant colonel smiled when McDonald walked into the brightly lit room. "It's really good to have you back." He held out his hand and shook the senior NCO's with sincere vigor. McDonald had been the best recon team leader CCN had ever produced, and he was missed.

"I don't know if I can say the same thing, sir." McDonald's eyes flashed around the room, absorbing every old detail.

"I can't say that you don't have cause . . . but things have changed here. . . . We've . . . ahhh . . . *broken up* the NVA spy operation."

"I heard about that, sir. What really puzzles me is how they could have done everything they did after they were neutralized: breaking into a parachute riggers' shed at Da Nang Air Base; stealing a C-130 and flying it to North Vietnam; parachuting out when they could have *landed* the aircraft and really become national heros over there."

"Yeah . . . that was weird . . . real weird." The lieutenant colonel shook his head in wonder. "But that's what war is all about. . . . Sometimes stupid mistakes can cost you."

McDonald took a seat. "So tell me, Colonel . . . what have you found out?"

"A *lot*. I don't think that we've ever had better intelligence on a POW camp location." The officer opened a medium-brown Army-issue leather courier's briefcase. The handcuff that the lieutenant colonel had removed earlier from his wrist bumped against the tabletop. McDonald watched the officer unbuckle one of the brass fasteners and then the other one. Something was going on that was extremely important, more important than a normal POW snatch. The officer removed a standard brown envelope and opened it. "Here; but before you look at it, I've got to warn you that the material is *very* emotional."

McDonald took the eight-by-ten black-and-white photograph and looked at it. A few seconds passed as he oriented the people in the photo. The person wearing only black pajama bottoms was hanging upside down from a bamboo pole and tied up in a bundle. The man wielding the bamboo cat-o'-nine-tails was black.

The CCN commander watched for a reaction from the sergeant, but was still taken by surprise when it came.

"James!" McDonald hissed between his teeth. *"James!"* He turned the photograph around until it was upside down and stared hard at the pain-twisted face of the soldier being tortured. "My God . . . oh my God . . . it's Barnett. . . ."

"Do you know these men?" The officer was shocked. He had not expected that McDonald would be personally familiar with the men in the secret photograph.

McDonald dropped the photo down on the table and stared across the room.

"Do you *know* these men?" The lieutenant colonel was becoming angry.

"Yes . . . I know both of them. They were students of mine at the Recondo School. . . ." McDonald felt tears oozing out of his eyes and getting trapped in the wrinkles. He didn't give a damn if the lieutenant colonel was angry or if he saw him crying. He didn't give a damn! "It's really ironic . . . fucking *ironic*!"

The CCN commander sensed that there was a lot more to McDonald's coming up to Command and Control North than met the eye. "What's so ironic?"

"Barnett rescued three American POWs when he was on patrol in the Ia Drang. He actually disobeyed orders to do it and risked his ass. . . . Now *he's* a POW in an NVA camp. . . ." McDonald picked the photograph back up and stared at Spencer's face. The old sergeant could almost hear the scream coming out of the soldier's mouth. "Do you know he's only seventeen years old? Seventeen!" McDonald kept staring at the picture. "He's a *baby*! And we have *senior* NCOs stacked up in supply rooms throughout this whole damn country, who are on medical profiles and can't fight or hump the jungle.... We send seventeen-year-olds out there instead."

McDonald's comment struck home with the field-grade officer. He had twin eighteen-year-old boys in college, and secretly he was glad that they had a college deferment and were protected from the draft. There was no way he wanted his boys fighting in this jungle. "What about this guy named James?"

McDonald snapped his head around and faced the officer. "He is a fucking traitor! And a murderer." The sergeant shifted his eyes from the officer back down to the picture. "There was an incident during the recondo class. Barnett, Woods, and James were all trainees. One night I went to the latrine and on the back of a *freshly* painted shitter door was written I KILL HONKIES. We thought someone was playing games, but I matched the handwriting against their bedding cards and reduced the suspects down to two men: James and a kid named Billy-Bob Fillmore. Billy-Bob was a southern white, and James came from Detroit—a black ghetto in Detroit. I almost got James to admit that he killed white soldiers on patrol, and there was an incident during the Recondo School's seven-day patrol where we ran into some NVA and I lost a man.... He was killed by an M-16, and James was the only one who had fired an M-16 during the firefight; Barnett had an M-60 and a couple of the others used M-79s, but no one but James had fired an *M-16*. James claimed that he saw a couple NVA carrying M-16s running through the jungle. I'm *sure* he shot the kid in the back. I reported the incident to the commandant, and he said that he would handle it because the implication was so awesome—blacks killing white Americans on patrol!" McDonald stopped talking and looked at the pleasure written on

James's face in the photograph. There was no way the photo could have been staged. James had turned coat and was helping the NVA!

"That's a really unbelievable story, Sergeant McDonald, and if anyone but you had told it to me, I would have called him a liar."

"There was a little doubt back during Recondo School, but I don't have *any* doubt now." McDonald's eyes narrowed. "We don't have any time to screw around. I need a team formed, and we had better start training *tonight*! If the NVA move Barnett before I can get there, I'll never forgive myself . . . *never*. This is one boy I'm not going to fail!" McDonald tapped the photograph hard with his index finger. "You tell your men that I don't need any candy-asses on this mission. . . . A prisoner snatch is difficult under the best of conditions, and this is going to be one nasty mess." McDonald stood up, signaling that he was done talking. He paused in the doorway and looked back over his shoulder at the commander. "When you pick your men, I don't want *any* married men with kids on this team . . . only *lean, mean* killers . . . killers all. I'm going to turn that camp into a meat market before a single NVA soldier can lift a finger." McDonald's voice lowered to a gravel rattle. "There aren't going to be any *throats cut this time!*"

The lieutenant colonel watched Master Sergeant McDonald leave the isolation building and jog over to the TOC. He was glad that the man was on his side. He didn't know why the old sergeant cared so much about this Barnett kid, but he knew that the young soldier couldn't have a better man to plan his rescue.

Sergeant Shaw slowed the vehicle down in front of his supply room. A military police jeep with an M-60 machine gun mounted in the back of it was parked next to the tent. Simpson started scrambling for the back of the truck over the wooden divider that separated the cab from the bed. Shaw reached up and pulled the black soldier back down on the seat.

"Don't fucking panic!" The supply sergeant's heart was pounding its way up his throat. He knew the load of supplies he was hauling was supported by bogus paperwork that wouldn't stand a cursory inspection, but what really worried him was the duffel bag full of heroin and marijuana that Simpson had picked up on their way back from his Vietnamese suppliers.

David Woods sat on the pallet of sundry packs and smiled; it was about time Shaw and Simpson paid their dues. A tall MP sergeant stepped out of the front screen door of the framed tent at the sound of the truck engine. He waved for the truck to pull over and park.

"I'm going to waste the motherfucker if he mentions a search!" Simpson flipped the safety switch off his M-16.

Woods directed the barrel of his CAR-15 around until it pointed at Simpson's back, which was separated from him only by a canvas divider. There would be no killing of any military policemen while he was on the truck.

"Is Specialist Woods on this truck?" the sergeant called up to Shaw.

The supply sergeant took a deep breath and released it before answering. "Yeah . . ." He pointed with his thumb to the rider in back.

The MP sergeant beckoned for Woods to hop down off the truck. Simpson pushed his safety back on and smiled over at Shaw. The MPs had been waiting for Woods and not them.

"You're wanted up at Brigade HQ . . . ASAP!" The sergeant led the way over to the jeep.

As soon as the MP jeep pulled away, Shaw fell against the steering wheel of the truck and closed his eyes. "Man! That was fucking close!"

"Shit! That wasn't *nothing*! When I worked for a gang in Detroit called Young Boys Incorporated, we used to deal right next door to a police precinct headquarters!" Simpson sighed. He had been scared too; he wasn't a teenager anymore, and getting busted would put him in jail. He was too rich for that kind of harassment.

* * *

Brigadier General Seacourt waited in the First Brigade commander's office. He had been briefed on Woods and Arnason by the senior brigade staff and had ordered that five members of the brigade's recon company be assigned to him for a special mission. They were waiting for Woods to return from his supply detail before leaving for Da Nang. The brigade commander was getting very nervous having the high-powered general waiting for a low-ranking enlisted man and had ordered the MPs to the tent to pick him up as soon as he arrived back from Da Nang. Seacourt had enjoyed the wait, talking to Sergeant Arnason about Barnett, James, and Woods. The general felt as if he already knew Specialist Woods when the young soldier walked into the operations bunker.

Woods looked around the crowded planning area and saw Arnason talking to a man who had his back facing the door. David went over to see what was going on from his sergeant and noticed that everyone in the bunker started staring at him. He reached down to feel if his fly was open.

"David!" Arnason looked over and saw him approaching. He waited until Woods stopped next to the officer before introducing him. "General, this is Specialist Woods."

David saw the black stars on the officer's collar at the exact instant Arnason had said the word *general*. Woods saluted.

"I've been waiting to meet you, Specialist." Seacourt returned the soldier's salute, even though they were indoors, and then held out his hand. David took it and shook, awkwardly. He felt very uncomfortable talking to a general.

Seacourt understood, and eased Woods out of his predicament. "Now that we're all here, let's load up."

Woods looked to Arnason for an explanation and received only a puzzled look.

"Don't worry about your gear. You'll be issued whatever you need when we get there, including weapons." Seacourt nodded to the captain who had accompanied him from Saigon.

Woods pressed his CAR-15 against his back using his elbow. The weapon hung upside down over his right shoulder. He wasn't going to part with it, even for a brigadier general.

Seacourt caught the gesture and smiled. "Of course, you can bring your weapons if you like."

"Where are we going, sir?" Sergeant Arnason asked the question as soon as the group had cleared the bunker.

"Da Nang . . . I'll brief you and your men when we get there as to what's going on. This mission will be voluntary, but once you're briefed, you'll have to stay in isolation until the rest of the men return—that is, if you decide not to go."

The small convoy of vehicles drove over to the runway and pulled up next to a parked CV-2 Caribou that was waiting to take off, its engines running and its tailgate dropped, ready to load up. General Seacourt led the way onto the aircraft and took a seat up near the cockpit. One of the crew offered the general a cup of coffee and the senior officer accepted, but he made sure that all of the men were offered something to drink before he took a sip from his Styrofoam cup.

Woods kept looking over at Arnason for some answers, but the team sergeant knew as little as David did. They settled back in the comfortable seats for the short ride to Da Nang. David looked out of the side window and could see Highway 1 winding through the green and brown hills below them. He had just made the long trip by road and was returning with a general on board. Woods wondered if this had something to do with Shaw's black-marketing and Simpson's drug-dealing. He twisted his mouth in thought and then shrugged his shoulders. He was clean.

Sergeant Arnason was also puzzled. He looked at the faces of the men the general had asked for by name: Lee San Ko, Kirkpatrick, Lieutenant Reed, and Woods. Including himself, four out of the five men had been on patrols together at A Shau.

CHAPTER FIVE

Run! Run!

Master Sergeant McDonald lay on the sand dune between two of the perimeter's fighting bunkers and listened to the sound of the South China Sea on the other side of the barbed wire. He had scooped up a pile of sand for a backrest and looked back over the wire with his legs stretched out in front of him. A cool breeze blew in across the water, but the sand was still warm from the afternoon sun and felt good against his back.

Thoughts, thousands and thousands of thoughts, filled his mind and covered the whole spectrum of human emotion. They moved at the speed of light down the electrical paths of his brain and connected with thoughts that he thought had been lost. Once they were joined, they created a montage of his life that wasn't in any chronological order. He thought about Project Cherry and then the Recondo School. He had been happy at the school and should have stayed there. No one in Vietnam would have held it against him to have stayed at the school. All he would have needed to say was that his wounds still hurt, and they would have understood. Deep, deep inside of him, where no one went but him, he felt the fear. He saw the POWs tied down on the planks and the blood soaking into the weathered wood. He could not bear to see Spencer Barnett like that, with the white cartilage of his vocal cords exposed to insects.

The soft vibrations of someone walking on the sand nearby brought McDonald back to the beach. He listened and could hear the sand spraying from the tips of the person's boots when the leather and rubber impacted with the loose grains. He would have to show whomever was coming how to walk on dry sand.

"Sergeant McDonald?" The voice was a whisper.

"Over here, Woods," McDonald kept watching the dark water roll against the beach. A white line indicated where the high-water mark was. He had been shocked to see Woods and the team from the First Cavalry arrive at CCN and was even more shocked when he heard that they would be a part of the team, including the lieutenant. They would all come under his command. It wasn't often that officers were placed under the operational control of enlisted men, but CCN did what needed to be done to get the mission accomplished, and everyone knew that Master Sergeant McDonald was the foremost expert of prisoner snatches in Vietnam. *They* knew that . . . but he didn't feel it.

"I got my stuff put up and thought you might enjoy some company out here." Woods sat down uninvited next to the sergeant. "I want to thank you for letting me stay on. . . . It means a lot to me."

"I know what you're saying, but I almost agreed with Lieutenant Nappa and Sergeant Cooper from RT Viper. . . . You're too emotionally involved and are dangerous because of it. We can't make *any* mistakes! *None!*"

"I promise, Sarge. . . . You tell . . . I do!" Woods held his hands up with his palms directed at the resting NCO. "I'm the one who left Spence back there and I've got to be a part of the team that gets him out. . . ."

"That part is understood. . . . No one questions your motivation, but you've got to remember that our going back in there is putting a lot of lives on the line . . . and there could be *more* POWs if we fuck up." McDonald didn't like his own choice of words, but it was true.

"I just came out here to tell you that you can count on me. I won't let you down, Sergeant!"

"Hell, Woods . . . I knew that back in Recondo School!" McDonald's white teeth shone in the moonlight. "Now get your ass back to the hooch and get some sleep. . . . It's going to be a very long day tomorrow and the next day."

"OK, Sarge . . ." Woods started back toward the hooch.

"Woods."

He stopped walking. "Yeah, Sarge?"

"Heel first when you're walking on sand . . . Toe first sends a spray out that can be heard by a deaf NVA whore!"

"Right, Sarge!" Woods paused and readjusted the way he was walking. "Are you coming?"

"No . . . If I'm needed, I'll be out here." McDonald slipped back into his thoughts almost instantly.

The telephone was ringing. He opened his eyes, but everything was still pitch black. He slowly oriented himself in the motel room and rolled over on the bed with his arm extended, fumbling for the receiver. It fell down and hit the carpeted floor. He could hear a voice saying hello and reached for the sound.

"Sergeant McDonald speaking." He whispered the words.

The voice of a North Carolina state trooper echoed in his ear. He was being told that his wife and teenage son had been killed in a head-on collision by a drunk driver. McDonald could hear the young trooper's voice echoing in his mind; not a single word of the conversation had been lost over the years.

The hardest thing he had ever done in his life was going to the mountain city morgue to identify his wife and son's bodies. They had his wife in a small refrigerated container at one end of the morgue and his thirteen-year-old son far away at the other end. He asked if they would move the boy's body and place it in the same cell as his mother's. The coroner's assistant refused, until McDonald convinced him that it would save all of them a lot of trouble if he would reconsider his decision. The coroner was called and a compromise was made, where they moved the small boy's body to the container next to his mother's.

McDonald felt the cool sea breeze against his cheeks. The sensation was amplified by the tears covering his cheeks. How he had loved them! They were the *perfect* military family and had even appeared as a family on the cover of *Army Times*. She had had the whole front page framed and had hung it on the wall of their living room. She would point to the picture when they had a fight or if their son was acting up and remind them that they were a *perfect* military family.

McDonald let his tears flow; it was the only way to put out the emotional fire that was burning in his heart.

She had never complained, no matter how bad things got, and living on a corporal's pay had been tough. He had worked nights as a bartender at the Officers' Club, and she had worked as a cook in the kitchen. He would catch her staring at him through the swinging doors that separated the kitchen from the main dining room and she would just smile. Their son was a love child, conceived in love and loved every second of his life by both of them. McDonald couldn't think of a single incident or time when he didn't see a smile on his son's face when the boy first saw him. He might have been gone only five minutes, but when he reappeared his son smiled a greeting. He had been a love child, and even though McDonald was only a sergeant in the military pecking order, as far as his son was concerned he was a five-star general about to be promoted.

Yes, he loved them, even though they were dead. The problem now was that Spencer Barnett looked *exactly* like his son; the same eyes, hair, body build, even the same shy smile.

The special POW recovery team had been training at CCN Headquarters for two weeks and had meshed into an excellent fighting force. The First Cavalry recon men and the CCN RT Viper team blended perfectly with only one minor problem, and that was to be expected. Lieutenant Reed didn't like the idea of coming under the operational control of a noncommissioned officer. Lieutenant Nappa from RT Viper had worked under a CCN sergeant when he had first come in-country and was training for his team, so he couldn't have cared less. Nappa knew McDonald's excellent reputation, and he also knew that most Special Forces sergeants were qualified to be officers and many of them had taken direct commissions. He had no problem with McDonald's leading the rescue team.

The team was composed of eight Americans and three Bru tribesmen who would act as scouts and interpreters. All of them carried CAR-15 submachine guns with thirty-round magazines that supplied a lot of firepower in highly concentrated bursts. They were issued Browning 9mm pistols that held a fourteen-round magazine as sidearms and specially designed survival knives. Each officer carried a Pen double-E camera, and every man had a transponder taped to his web gear on one harness and a flashing strobe light taped to the opposite side. The team was designed for fighting; they carried only ammunition and grenades. If they became separated and had to escape and evade the enemy, they would have to get their food from the jungle using the compact survival packs on their pistol belts.

McDonald walked down the line of gear laid out on the isolation-hooch floor. He inspected each piece of equipment to ensure that it worked.

"Cooper, I think we had better carry two bolt cutters, just in case. . . ." McDonald tested the cutter as he talked.

"I agree; they might have them all chained up, and two would make things faster."

"There is probably a South Vietnamese POW camp nearby. . . . The NVA usually keep the Americans and South Vietnamese separate and chain the ARVN soldiers to posts."

McDonald paused in front of Kirkpatrick's gear and looked directly into the eyes of the soldier from New York. "You sure you feel you can make it?"

"The doctors said that I was as good as new. Besides . . . I owe them for killing my buddy Brown."

Woods listened. Brown and Kirkpatrick had both been with him on the recon patrol that buried the new secret seismic-intrusion detectors. Kirkpatrick had been wounded and Brown killed in the NVA ambush. The two black New

Yorkers had been inseparable and had been working with Sergeant Shaw black-marketeering supplies. Kirkpatrick had changed after Brown's death. He was now the perfect recon man: all business.

Woods watched the Special Forces men during the inspection. Sergeant Cooper was about his own age and had gone through the extensive Green Beret training, graduating with honors. The lieutenant was different from line unit officers in that he would talk *to* enlisted men and not down to them. That seemed to be a leadership trait with most Special Forces officers and was probably based on the extremely high caliber of NCOs found on their teams.

McDonald finished checking the last man's gear and turned at the end of the row of equipment to face back down the line. "Looks good. We insert the day after tomorrow. I want you to leave your gear here in the isolation hooch. Tonight is your last free night, and then we'll all be restricted to this building for our final briefings and orders." McDonald pointed at Woods and Cooper. "You two come with me. We've got to drive over to Twenty-fourth Headquarters and pick up some maps."

Woods and Cooper followed their team sergeant to the exit, and each one of them took a CAR-15 out of the weapons rack next to the door and a thirty-round magazine out of the ammo box on the floor. The weapons were there for exactly that purpose—to be used as loaners. Once a team's weapons had been inspected for a patrol, they stayed in the building. Perfection was the key to success, and every one of the team's weapons had been inspected by the CCN armorer and cleaned thoroughly before being reassembled. Any doubtful part had been replaced with a new one and then tested.

Cooper drove the black jeep and McDonald rode shotgun. Woods sat on the jump seat with his CAR-15 across his legs. The traffic was heavy once they pulled out onto Highway 1, heading north to the large American headquarters complex. A long convoy of five-ton flatbed trucks lined the road carrying ammunition to units in the southern part of the Corps.

Most of the really heavy traffic was heading south on the road, but that would change in a couple of hours when the trucks from the fire support bases took to the roads after the engineer mine-sweeping details had finished.

Woods watched a herd of water buffalo wallowing in the thick rice-paddy mud. The herd boy stood on the side of the road holding a long, flexible stick. He called out for a cigarette as they passed, and Woods pulled three Kools out of his pack and threw them on the side of the highway. The boy ran smiling after them.

James walked through the front doors of the Corps operations complex carrying a briefcase in one hand. He wore a pistol belt and a .45-caliber pistol at his side. The military police guard just inside the doors looked up from his desk and smiled a greeting at the black "captain."

"Morning, sir." The MP thought the captain was a bit young-looking, but in Vietnam, officer promotions were so rapid anything was possible. "Can I help you?"

"Yes, soldier. Direct me to the plans section, please." James flexed his jaws.

"Down the hall to the left and then make another left. It'll be the first double doors on your left." The MP pointed with his gloved finger.

"Left, left, and left. I should be able to remember that set of directions. Thank you." James started walking through the gate.

"Sir, I'll need some identification." The MP looked at the captain's briefcase. "And I'll have to check your case."

"I am in a hurry, soldier. . . ." James laid his briefcase on the small table that had been provided for that purpose and opened the latches. He lifted the cover, and a red cover sheet flashed into view that had SECRET printed on it.

The MP glanced at the papers and looked back at the captain. "Thank you, sir."

James closed the briefcase and started leaving.

"Sir . . . I need to see some identification." The MP's voice was losing its patience.

James reached into his rear pocket and produced his wallet. He flipped it open and laid it on the table in front of the MP. A green-and-white military ID card with James's photograph was displayed behind a plastic cover.

The MP lifted the wallet and looked at the card. "You've got to get your ID updated; it says that you're a lieutenant."

James smiled. "I just got promoted...*ahead* of my peers."

"Thank you, sir!" The MP handed James back his wallet and let him pass.

James walked down the hall, thinking how dumb whites were. They would believe anything, absolutely anything. He watched the signs above the doors as he passed and tried memorizing them for future visits to the headquarters complex. He had been to the First Marine Division Headquarters before and had no problem getting past the black guard on duty there. The Marine had been very impressed meeting a black captain. James smiled. Maybe next time he would be a major, or maybe a lieutenant colonel.

A large stained sign was nailed above the double doors with PLANS burned into the wood. A cardboard sign on each side of the doors warned that only authorized entry was allowed. James didn't hesitate and walked through the swinging door.

The large room was a beehive of activity. Maps covered all of the walls, and officers and senior NCOs from all of the XXIV Corps units were busy making overlays from the Corps battle plans. James looked for the map that depicted the junction of Laos, South Vietnam, and North Vietnam. He saw the map on the wall and started walking toward it when another captain reached up and grabbed him by the arm.

"Where in the fuck do you think you're going, stud?"

James twisted away and glared at the heavyset officer. "To trace an overlay...cunt!"

"You can't just fucking walk in here and make overlays!" The officer had been up all night and was very tired and angry. He had missed breakfast.

"What would you like for me to do?" James was getting nervous.

"Sign the fucking logbook!" The captain pointed to the open ledger. "You fucking field jocks think you can just fucking ignore procedures!"

James picked up the pen that was attached by a string to the book and signed his name: Martin Luther King, Jr.

The other captain turned the ledger around and read what James had written. "Funny . . . real fucking funny!"

"Hey, man . . . can't you take a joke?" James picked up the pen again and wrote the name that was on his ID card: Ben Arnold.

The captain smiled when he read the name. "I'd use Martin Luther King too if my name was Benedict Arnold."

"*Ben* Arnold . . . *Ben!* Do you want to see my ID card?" James glared at his cover peer.

The captain thought for a second before answering. "No . . . but there's something about you that I don't like. . . ."

James felt his heart beat faster.

"Go on and make your overlays!" The staff captain nodded in the direction of the battle maps. "I've been up all night posting that shit, so it's the latest stuff going!"

"Thank you, *sir*." James walked over to the I Corps Vietnam map and smiled. A new Marine and Army combined operation had been posted in blue grease pencil. He pushed his fatigue cap to the back of his head and taped the transparent paper over the battle plans. James took a half-hour copying the data and unit locations. He wished that he could also get a copy of the operations orders, but that would be risking too much.

A Marine lieutenant colonel watched James work. There was something about the way the Army captain carried himself that bothered him. He knew that a lot of blacks had been pushed through the Army OCS programs and through ROTC because of the aggressive equal-opportunity programs, but they must have really been hurting when they commissioned him. The man's whole attitude reeked of street punk, not officer. The lieutenant colonel looked at James's cap riding on the back of his head over a sprouting Afro hairdo.

James folded the overlay and looked at the map on the wall behind him. A large block-letter sign read TOP SECRET on the black vinyl drape covering the battle plan. James looked slowly around the room and saw that the captain who had given him a hassle when he had entered was gone. He smiled and decided to risk it. James picked up another piece of overlay paper and some paper tape and approached the top-secret map. He had lifted a corner of the vinyl cover and was trying to pin it back when a heavy hand grabbed him by his shoulder.

"What do you think you're doing!" The Marine lieutenant colonel pulled James around until the black soldier was facing him. "Can't you read? That's a top-secret battle plan with a special 'need to know.'. . . Do you have clearance?"

"Yes sir! I'm supposed to get copies of everything in the I Corps Tactical Zone. . . ." James tried bluffing his way.

"Who said the plan was in I Corps?" The lieutenant colonel wasn't about to be bullshitted.

"I just assumed."

"An assumption is the mother of a fuck-up, Captain . . . and you just fucked up. Now get out of here." The more the Marine office looked at James, the madder he got. The captain was just too arrogant.

"Sure . . . sir." James dropped his eyes down to the floor. "I didn't mean to cause you any trouble."

"You have . . . now move your ass!" The Marine looked James's shoulders for a unit patch and saw that there wasn't any sewn on. "What unit you from?"

James hesitated before answering, "The Cav."

"What *unit*, Captain?"

"First Brigade, Recon Company, First Cavalry Division, Airmobile . . . *sir!*"

"Don't be a smartass, Captain, or I'll have the MPs escort you out of here!"

"Yes sir!"

The Marine lieutenant colonel turned away in disgust. He

was going to mention the captain to the Army general he worked for. He didn't care what the general did about it, but he wasn't going to work for the Army and take shit from junior officers. "What's your name, soldier?"

"James—" James caught himself. "Ben Arnold, sir."

"James Ben Arnold?" The lieutenant colonel became very suspicious. He sensed something was very wrong. "Let me see your ID card."

James removed his wallet and pulled his NVA-forged ID card from the protector and handed it to the officer.

The Marine looked at the picture and down at the card a half-dozen times before staring at James, who looked away. "You stay here. I'm going to have the MPs check you out. There's something very fishy about you."

James felt his stomach turn sour and squeezed his left upper arm against his side to make sure the 9mm pistol was still there. He had checked his .45 in with the MP at the duty desk according to Corps procedures.

"Sir! We need you right away in the general's briefing room! It's important. Brigadier General Seacourt is in there, and they want you."

The Marine lieutenant colonel looked down at the ID card and back at James. "Here! And the next time I see you, you'd better have a decent haircut!" He handed the card back to James and hurried after the staff lieutenant.

James left the plans room and stopped out in the hallway to catch his breath. That had been too close a call. He felt the sweat running down his sides. His eyes focused and he read the sign with the black arrow pointing to the left that showed the direction of the snack bar. He felt hungry after all of the pressure and decided on having something to eat before heading back to his camp. He had already lined up a helicopter ride out to the Marine forward base called The Rockpile. He could walk to his contact point from there.

The Vietnamese woman who operated the counter at the snack bar took the ten-dollar MPC note from James and paused to look at the dark brown spot that covered a third of

the bill. She didn't know if she should take the damaged
money and called the club NCO over to her counter.

The staff sergeant looked at the note and then at James.
"What happened to it?"

"You got me, Sarge; I got it from the PX like that. . . .
Maybe somebody spilled some paint or ink on it." James
shrugged his shoulders.

The sergeant looked at the MPC certificate again and
frowned. He handed it to the woman. "Take it."

James took his tray and found a seat near the wall. He
knew the stain was dried blood from the American soldier's
body it had been removed from by the NVA.

The longer James sat there eating, the more pissed he
became. He had told Lieutenant Van Pao that the cover name
Ben Arnold would cause more problems than the insult was
worth, but she had insisted his ID card and other papers have
that name on them. She found the name of the American
Revolutionary War traitor a perfect form of irony for James's
cover. He was going to cause some hell when he returned to
the camp over the money with dried blood on it; there was
no excuse for that kind of carelessness—none!

Woods sat in the armchair outside of the office. McDonald
was in with Sergeant Cooper. Brigadier General Seacourt
was inside the room with them getting briefed on the POW
snatch operation. He had been in there, but all of the cigar
smoke was making him sick, so he slipped outside to catch
his breath. Besides, there wasn't anything going on in there
that he didn't know by heart.

A command sergeant major walked by and then stopped
and backed up. "There's a small snack bar right around the
corner if you want a soda or a hamburger, young man."

"Thanks, Sergeant Major." Woods nodded and smiled.

"No problem. The hamburgers are *good*, though. . . ." He
patted his stomach. "Too good!"

Woods looked over at the closed door and figured they
would be in there a few more minutes, long enough for him
to get something to eat. He stopped by one of the clerk's

desks before leaving and asked the guy to tell McDonald where he had gone in case they came out early.

James finished his food and stepped out of the door into the hallway. He looked to his left and saw the exit door leading out onto the quadrangle and the parked staff vehicles. He figured he could hitch a ride to the Marine helipad easily enough. Whites were stupid.

Woods turned the corner and saw James staring directly at him. He stopped and blinked his eyes. It was James, but he was wearing captain's bars on his cap and collar.

"James!" The single word coming out of Woods's throat echoed down the narrow hall like a cannon shot.

James turned away from his ex-teammate and hurried to the exit door. Once he stepped outside, he started running as fast as he could. His briefcase smashed against his leg.

Woods took a few seconds before he reacted. He was sure the officer was James, but the way the black officer had reacted, he could have been wrong. He put his hand on the snack bar door and paused. He was *sure* the man was James; he was *sure!* Woods hurried down the hallway to the exit and stepped outside. The black officer was gone. He walked a few steps toward the parked vehicles and then changed his mind. Maybe the officer just looked like James. He had been thinking a lot lately about the ambush and the A Shau Valley, where James had been with them. He was probably just seeing things. The smell of frying hamburgers drew him back inside and over to the snack bar.

Cooper kept twisting his lips as they drove back to the CCN compound. He was deep in thought and drove the jeep slower than he normally did. McDonald kept his eyes locked on the Vietnamese houses lining the right-hand side of the road.

Woods kept playing with the selector switch on his CAR-15, flicking it on and off full automatic. A dozen times he started to tell McDonald about what had happened at the XXIV Corps snack bar, but each time he stopped himself.

McDonald turned around sideways on the canvas seat and looked back at Woods. "You know, *everyone* gets nervous before they go out on patrol. . . . This mission is no different, Woods."

Woods stopped flicking the selector switch and decided that he was going to tell the sergeant and take the ribbing. "It's not the mission, Sarge. . . . I—I saw a captain who looked like . . . James." Woods shook his head and corrected himself. "You might think I'm fucking crazy . . . but . . . it *was* James, dressed up like a captain!" Woods couldn't believe what he had just said to McDonald.

McDonald stared hard at Woods and frowned. "Are you sure?"

"Sarge, I told you that you'd think I'm fucking crazy. . . . I know what James looks like, but man, you know his . . . *eyes*." Woods swallowed. "Someone can look *like* James, but nobody can have the same look in his eyes."

McDonald knew exactly what Woods was saying. "Turn around!" He grabbed Cooper's arm. "*Turn around . . . now!*"

The drive back to Corps Headquarters took them half the time it had taken getting there the first time. Cooper wove between the traffic like a Philippine taxi driver. He paused at the main gates to the complex just long enough to get checked in. The MP remembered them from earlier, because of the black-painted jeep, and rushed them through the checkpoints.

McDonald entered the exit door first, followed closely by Woods. "Where did you see him?" McDonald turned to face Woods.

"He was standing over there by the snack bar door." Woods pointed and McDonald ran to the spot.

The master sergeant looked inside the bar, hoping that James would have returned, and saw only a couple of staff officers drinking coffee. He turned to leave and his eyes locked on a stained sign hanging above a closed door: PLANS. Everything fell together for him as he ran to the door and entered the classified area. The duty captain stopped him at the door and asked for his ID. McDonald produced it and at the same time scanned the room and the maps hanging on all of the walls. He was sure now.

"Did a black captain—say, in his early twenties—come in here this afternoon?" McDonald felt his breath catch in his throat.

"Hey, Sergeant . . . do you know how many officers pass through here in one day?" The captain looked at McDonald as if he were nuts to ask such a dumb question.

"It's very important, sir! *Very* important!" The tone in McDonald's voice drew the attention of a Marine lieutenant colonel who had been reading a complex battle plan. The officer looked up from his desk and recognized the sergeant who had been in the briefing earlier with General Seacourt. "Sergeant McDonald?"

"Yes sir . . ." McDonald left the duty officer's desk and went over to the lieutenant colonel's, followed closely by Woods.

"Did you say a black captain?"

"Yes sir . . . thin . . . about twenty years old . . . *hard* eyes."

"Does he have a budding Afro hairdo?"

"Could be . . ."

"He was here, right before the meeting with General Seacourt. I was going to have the MPs run a check on him, but the meeting took precedence."

"Shit! If only you would have!" McDonald slapped the lieutenant colonel's desk. "Shit!"

"What's going on?"

McDonald looked around the room. "Did he get any op orders? Overlays? Anything!"

"I watched him copy the battle plan of the I Corps map, and then he went over there to copy the top-secret op plan, and I stopped him." The officer pointed to the black vinyl with the red letters stenciled on it and the cardboard sign above it.

"That's our plan?" McDonald questioned the officer.

"Yes."

A cold chill slipped down McDonald's spine. "Did he see it . . . even for a second?"

"I doubt it. He lifted the bottom corner and I stopped him."

"Come and show me." McDonald led the way over to the map that had the POW snatch laid out on it.

The lieutenant colonel lifted the corner of the cover a little higher than James had and looked at the sergeant.

"Hold it right there." McDonald squatted down and viewed all of the map that had been exposed. It showed the lower half of Laos, with a bit of the operational area exposed. "Man, that's risky!"

"What in the hell is going on?" The Marine lieutenant colonel was confused and getting angry over being kept in the dark.

"James . . . or . . . what did he call himself?"

The Marine thought for a second, and then a light came on in his eyes. "He called himself James at first! Then he caught himself and said his name was . . ." The officer's eyes opened wide as he realized the irony in the name he was about to say. "Ben Arnold."

"He's got a set of brass balls!" McDonald looked at Woods and shook his head. "James was captured by the NVA only a few months ago . . . less than that . . . and we think he's turned coat. He's working as an NVA spy and saboteur."

"What was his rank?"

"Specialist Fourth Class . . . why?"

"I *knew* there was something about him that didn't make sense. . . . He wore captain's bars, but didn't *act* like a captain." The Marine officer wrinkled his lips until they turned white. "I should have followed my gut instincts!"

McDonald looked at the Marine officer and grinned. "We might just make this work for us, sir. If the NVA know our op plans, they might just take *advantage* of that opportunity . . . right?"

The officer took only a second to grasp what McDonald was leading up to. "You're right! We can change the plans and be waiting for the NVA to attack our *weakest* points."

The lieutenant colonel nodded his head. "Good work, Sergeant!"

"It was Specialist Woods who saw him." McDonald gave the credit to the young soldier.

"Well, there will be some kind of award for this! A lot of American lives have been saved, plus a traitor exposed, and I hate to think how much damage James could have done! I mean, nobody would ever suspect a *black* soldier. A white GI could be mistaken for a Frenchman gone renegade, but a black soldier could go just about anywhere in this country and never be questioned for being there."

"I'd get the word out to the rest of the planning people in the other Corps if I were you, sir." McDonald turned to leave.

"Believe me! By tomorrow night, James's picture will be in the hands of every commander in Vietnam. . . . He won't be able to show his face to an American again!"

James ran behind the building and stopped to check if Woods had followed him. He saw his ex-teammate pause near the row of vehicles and then go back inside the building. Sweat dripped off his chin. He waited until his breathing slowed down before walking over to the helipad. He had to get out of Da Nang as soon as possible.

The noise from a jet engine reached him, and he started running again. A Huey slick was starting to warm up. James ran over to the crew chief and asked where they were headed, and the man told him Con Thien and then out to Khe Sanh, a new area the Marines were opening up. James asked if they were going to stop at the Rockpile, and the crew chief ran over and asked the pilot, who was a black warrant officer.

The pilot beckoned James to come over to his window and yell above the noise of the engine so James could hear him. "Hop *on board . . . I'll drop you off!*"

James gave the brother a thumbs-up and scrambled onto the nylon mesh seat. He kept looking back for Woods until the skids left the ground, and then he relaxed against the seat and smiled as he patted his briefcase that contained the overlays of the big combined arms operation. There was going to be a number of surprises during that operation that the Americans would never forget!

CHAPTER SIX

Fool's Gold Escape

The hut was clean and smelled of freshly split bamboo and new thatch. Colonel Garibaldi looked down at the woven mats covering the floor and saw that they were also new. The hut had never been used before. There were two cots, one at each end of the ten-by-eight-foot building. The only sign that the hut housed POWs was the chain with the leg brackets that was attached to one of the main bamboo poles next to each bed.

"Look at this!" Barnett held up the new metal plate in one hand and the knife, fork, and spoon in his other hand.

"Something is going on that doesn't make any sense." Garibaldi shook his head. "First, the new hooch with a roof!" He looked up at the shade-producing cover and closed his eyes in silent prayer. "It's going to feel good sleeping at night and not get rained on or bake all day in the sun."

"Why do you think they're doing this?" Spencer sat down on his cot.

"I don't know. . . ." Colonel Garibaldi sat down across from the soldier. "I've been in a half-dozen of their POW camps, and I've never even heard of them allowing two prisoners to live together, much less given them all of these luxury items!" Garibaldi let his eyes sweep over the new blankets, eating utensils, spare clothes, water cans, and even a wash basin with a mirror attached to the wall of the hut.

"Well, I don't know what they've got planned, but I'm going to enjoy it while it lasts!" Spencer stretched out on the bamboo-framed cot that had been padded with thatch.

Colonel Garibaldi jumped to his feet. "Someone is coming. . . ."

Lieutenant Van Pao stepped through the low doorway and entered the hut smiling. She was followed by a small man wearing steel-frame glasses and carrying a dark brown leather satchel. "How are my Americans feeling today?" Van Pao's smile spread out over her face.

"Very good, ma'am." Colonel Garibaldi tilted forward slightly as a sign of respect and submission. He knew how to play the survival game well.

Barnett started getting up off his cot, but Van Pao stopped him by holding out her hand. "You may stay there, Spencer Barnett." She had begun calling him by both of his names since he had survived the whole night in Mother Kaa's cage without screaming even once. "Dr. Tam is going to examine you and the colonel and see if you need any special medical attention." She motioned for the North Vietnamese doctor to start examining Barnett.

The doctor used Van Pao as an interpreter and asked numerous questions about his health and how he was feeling as he conducted the examination. He had Spencer strip down to his new black pajama pants and checked his heart rate and lungs. The doctor barked a set of orders and looked at the lieutenant. She smiled and closed her eyes halfway before translating the order into English. "He wants you to stand up and lower your pants."

Spencer didn't hesitate. He wasn't going to give Sweet Bitch a second of pleasure by acting modest in front of her. He knew that she often hid near the POW latrine pit and watched them relieve themselves. She had a definite problem. Colonel Garibaldi had told him earlier that he thought she secretly wished she were a man and was extremely jealous of male sex organs.

The doctor gently squeezed Barnett's testicles and spoke sharply in Vietnamese to Van Pao. She shrugged her shoulders and spoke in a very respectful tone to the doctor and then asked Barnett, "Did you have a recent *accident* where you bruised your organs?"

Barnett glared at the lieutenant and knew that if he spoke the truth she would change it to what she wanted in translating to the doctor. He nodded his head in the affirmative. The doctor had been watching his face and could read the expression. He asked another question, and Van Pao translated it.

"Have you been passing blood with your urine?"

Spencer nodded yes.

"Is there pain when you urinate?"

Spencer nodded his head again.

"Do your testes hurt?"

Spencer paused before answering and shook his head no, even though they still throbbed from the beating he had received.

The doctor opened his bag and removed a hypodermic needle and gave Spencer seven shots from different bottles of medicine.

"You see, Spencer Barnett, the People's Army takes very good care of its prisoners of war." Lieutenant Van Pao lifted a fork off the small shelf. "How do you people eat with these things? Don't you stick yourselves?"

Barnett stared at the North Vietnamese officer without answering her. The doctor handed Spencer a tube of ointment for the soles of his feet and a roll of gauze.

Spencer looked directly into the eyes of the medical man and spoke in English. "Thank you." The universal tone of voice that spoke gratitude did not need translation. The doctor gave Spencer a curt nod and left to examine Colonel Garibaldi.

Lieutenant Van Pao kept watching Spencer while Garibaldi was being examined. She was trying to figure a way to break him before the division intelligence officer arrived. She had very little time left.

The doctor gave Colonel Garibaldi a large bottle of vitamin C and the same series of vitamin-B shots that he had given to Spencer, except for the dose of penicillin Spencer had been given to fight the numerous infections he was suffering from.

Colonel Garibaldi waited until the Vietnamese left the small hut and then handed Spencer some of the vitamin-C tablets.

"You keep them, Colonel." Barnett knew the officer was suffering from scurvy.

"There's plenty more in the bottle, and if you don't have some vitamin C, you'll end up losing your teeth too!"

Spencer accepted the gift and thanked the colonel. He chewed one of the tablets slowly and tasted the acid. It reminded him of a certain brand of candy that he would buy when he had gone to the movies as a little kid.

The sun was setting, and the old Montagnard entered the POW compound carrying a bucket of hot food. His grandson walked next to him as a guide and also to carry a bucket of rice wine. The old man set the bucket down on the small porch of the raised hut and waited for the Americans to come out.

Spencer was the first one out, carrying his tin plate, followed by the colonel. The old man lifted the lid and Spencer's breath caught in his throat. He could see the large hunks of boiled fish and the yellow pieces of egg in the rice.

"Shit, sir! Look at that!"

Garibaldi looked over Spencer's shoulder, but he had already smelled the food and knew that it was something more than the normal boiled rice without even salt added. "Something *is* going on!"

"Fuck them! As long as they want to mess with my mind like this, I don't give a fuck!" Spencer used his spoon to pile his plate high with the wholesome food.

The boy held up the container of rice wine. Garibaldi lifted the lid and smelled the fermenting juice. "I am going to wake up shortly and find out that we're eating monkey shit and drinking elephant piss!"

The boy smiled and motioned with his hands that they were to keep the whole container of wine.

Barnett caught hold of himself before the Montagnards left, and using the food containers to block the view of anyone watching them from the guard hut or from the thick vegetation on the other side of the fence, he made the motion of a knife cutting on his wrist and looked at the boy. The nine-year-old smiled and nodded his head once. He had understood.

Garibaldi carried the wine and Spencer carried the tin of food back into their new hut. They were going to feast and get drunk, very drunk, while the dream lasted.

James and Lieutenant Van Pao watched the Montagnards leave the small American compound through the small spy hole she had cut in the side of her office hut.

"Well?" Van Pao asked James to comment.

"Very good! You'll see that it will pay off when she arrives here tomorrow afternoon with the general."

"It had better! We've wasted good medicine on them! The doctor was so angry when he left that he said he was going to send a message to Hanoi personally! He has troops dying because there isn't enough penicillin, and he had to waste it on Spencer Barnett!"

"Believe me... *You'll* get a letter from Hanoi rewarding you for your excellent service!" James took a sip from his glass of Johnny Walker Black. "I'm going to visit them."

"Make sure you don't say anything to mess up tomorrow's visit!" Van Pao glared at James. He was becoming too powerful with the senior officers. His latest mission at Da Nang had cemented his trust with the top generals, and there was even talk of giving him a commission in the People's Army!

James waited until he couldn't hear the sound of the metal forks against the plates inside the hut before entering the compound. Garibaldi was lifting a cup of Montagnard rice wine to his mouth when he stepped through the door. James held a half-empty bottle of Johnny Walker Black in his left hand and an almost empty glass in his right. "A toast, Colonel?"

Garibaldi paused and then poured his cup of wine out on the floor.

"Dumb! But you can do what you want with your booze.... Me ... I'm going to drink mine." James sipped noisily from his glass and then smacked his lips. "Good stuff."

Spencer glared at the traitor from his seat on his cot.

"Well, Spence! How are you doing today? Better, I hope!" James held his glass to his mouth and smiled before taking another sip. His eyes were colder than a cobra's. He was getting in with the NVA generals, and as soon as his reputation was secure with them, he was going to ask for Spencer Barnett.

The question burned inside of Spencer, and even though he hated to talk to James, he had to ask. "Where do you get all that stuff?"

James acted as if Spencer's voice came out of the sky. He looked up at the ceiling and barked, "A voice! I hear a voice!"

"Knock off the bullshit, James.... Where do you come up with Marlboro cigarettes and American booze out here in the jungle?"

James removed his pack of cigarettes. "Kools ... Kool 100s ... is my brand."

Barnett was finished talking and sipped from his cup of Montagnard wine.

"So you really want to know?" James lit a Kool and inhaled deeply before answering Barnett. "Really, it's simple. A matter of *greed*, but that's the *American way* ... isn't it, Colonel?" He looked over at Garibaldi, who sat on the edge of his cot holding his empty cup upside down. James shrugged. "Do you remember guys like Sergeant Shaw?" James waited for Barnett to acknowledge his question.

Barnett nodded.

"Guys like Shaw black-market ... *anything*. Like I said, it's all a matter of greed. They think they're selling to crooked *South* Vietnamese, but actually they're selling to *our* agents." James drained his glass and poured it full again. "Does that answer your question?"

Barnett nodded.

"Oh! I almost forgot to tell you! I saw your old buddy yesterday in Da Nang. . . ." James walked over and refilled Garibaldi's cup with Johnny Walker Black. "If you pour that out, I'll have them cut your nuts off! Now drink, *Colonel!*"

Garibaldi obeyed. He raised the cup to his lips and sipped the scotch. He felt like crying. Scotch had been his favorite drink. The taste and smell brought back a flood of memories: his wife, the Officers' Club at Seymour Johnson Air Force Base in North Carolina, parties . . . happy times.

Barnett waited for James to continue talking. He was curious as to whom James was referring to.

"You know, this is a good life here at A Rum. I've got me a tight hole, good food, plenty of money. . . ."

Garibaldi knew where the money was coming from and felt the scotch in his mouth turn bitter.

"Did I tell you that they're thinking of making me an *officer*? A real officer in the People's Army." James sipped from his glass and raised his eyebrows. "I'm good, you know . . . real good at what I do!"

Barnett felt his hopes drop. He really wanted to know who James had seen in Da Nang.

"Woods!" James stomped his foot on the mat and pointed at Barnett. "Gotcha! You thought I forgot what I was talking about, didn't you!" James was getting drunk. "I saw your fucking buddy Woods back at the XXIV Corps Headquarters!"

Garibaldi acted as if he weren't paying any attention to James, but he was absorbing every word that he said. He held the cup of scotch in both hands, pretending it was a rare treat.

"Now ask me, *Spence*. . . . What was I doing at the XXIV Headquarters yesterday?"

Barnett glanced over at Garibaldi, and he nodded for him to ask.

"What were you doing at the XXIV Corps Headquarters yesterday?"

"*Sir!*" James glared at Barnett. "*Say sir!*"

"Sir."

"That's better." James set the empty glass down and drank directly from the open bottle. "I was getting overlays off the Corps battle maps." James enjoyed the conversation, and it made him feel good to brag about his exploits. Barnett and Garibaldi would appreciate how much guts it took to pull off what he had done. "I just walked right in there and copied their battle plans for the next month! I must say they're a bunch of dumb motherfuckers!"

"When did you see David?"

"Oh! You want to talk some more. . . . That wine must have loosened your white motherfuckin' tongue!" James staggered to his feet. "Well, *fuck you!*" He left the hut, bumping against the sides of the door and missing the ladder.

Barnett smiled when he heard James cuss as he hit the ground after falling off the three-foot-high porch.

Garibaldi waited until James was out of the compound. They could hear him cussing as he walked back to his hooch in the dark. "Oh, damn! This scotch is *so* good!" Garibaldi hugged the cup.

Spencer found the whole act extremely funny and started laughing. The Montagnard wine was having its effect.

Colonel Garibaldi stared at the seventeen-year-old soldier. It was the first time he had heard the boy laugh, and then he thought about himself. He hadn't laughed in *years*.

The sun had been up for hours. The Montagnard boy entering the hut woke Barnett from his deep sleep. Garibaldi struggled up on one elbow. They were both still drunk. The small boy picked up the night pot in the corner and noticed that it had been used only to urinate in. He carried it to the doorway and paused to look back at Barnett. The boy spoke a brief sentence in Bru and left.

Barnett struggled to his feet and then dropped back down on the cot. He felt like shit. The wine had been good the night before, but he was paying for it now.

"It must be mid-morning!" Garibaldi looked out of the door. "They let us sleep in! This is unbelievable!"

"Enjoy it!" Barnett felt like puking but fought the urge. He wasn't going to waste any of the food that he had eaten the night before.

The Montagnard boy returned from emptying the night pot and set the earthenware pot back down in the corner. A North Vietnamese guard waited in the doorway for the boy to finish. Barnett smiled at the nine-year-old who had helped him when he had been beaten and placed in the cage with Mother Kaa. The boy smiled back and nodded at the night pot before slipping out of the door.

Barnett didn't catch the meaning of the nod.

Garibaldi went out on the tiny porch and looked around the camp to see if there was any activity. He saw the normal guards in their thatch-covered hooches and noticed that all of them were wearing new uniforms.

"Something is going on today, Spencer." Garibaldi went back over to his cot.

"I feel like shit!" Barnett held his head with both hands.

"Montagnard wine does that to you . . . powerful stuff." Garibaldi looked over at the night pot and frowned. "I wonder if they're going to let us out of here today."

"Why?"

"I've got to defecate and I don't want to use the night pot if I don't have to." Garibaldi felt his stomach roll and knew that he wouldn't be able to hold it for more than a couple of minutes more. "Damn, I've got to go!"

Barnett struggled to his feet and went out on the porch to give the colonel a little privacy.

Garibaldi went over to the corner and untied the drawstring of his peasant pants. He looked in the pot before squatting over it and was glad that he did; two eight-inch-long Montagnard knives were inside the smelly container.

* * *

Lieutenant Van Pao waited on the edge of the jungle clearing with two of the camp guards. She was nervous and knew that when the helicopter landed, her future career could go either way. The sound of the helicopter approaching startled her, even though she was expecting it. The guards quickly checked their uniforms and shouldered their AK-47s.

The helicopter came in low and dropped down on the short grass in the clearing the Montagnards used to graze their animals. A North Vietnamese general and two Americans got out of the chopper, and Lieutenant Van Pao hurried to report to her division commander and his guests. The chopper crew pulled the camouflage netting from its storage place and quickly covered the aircraft before finding cool spots at the edge of the jungle to smoke and wait for their commander.

Van Pao saluted the general and smiled a greeting to the Americans. "It is a pleasure having you visit my small POW camp."

The American female smiled and looked over at her manager. "She speaks English; how nice."

"A lot of people do, my dear." The American celebrity's manager was hot and bored. He hadn't wanted her to take this trip out into the damn jungle, but she had insisted.

"Yes, I learned English at the University of Hanoi." Van Pao glanced over at the general for approval. "Let me show you the way." She took the lead down the trail to the Montagnard village. "I have two American POWs here at A Rum and fifty-three South Vietnamese and Montagnard CIDG prisoners."

"Let's skip them and show us the Americans. . . ." The starlet's manager was worried about being so close to the South Vietnamese border. He was too rich to get himself killed fucking around a war zone.

"If you like." Van Pao hid her hate.

Garibaldi and Barnett were sitting in the shade of their hut when the NVA party and their guests arrived outside the gate.

Colonel Garibaldi was the first one to see the visitors. "I know why they moved us to this hut."

"Why?" Barnett looked up at the colonel. He had his back facing the gate to the small American POW compound.

"Look behind you." Garibaldi's voice got lower with each word.

Spencer turned and watched Sweet Bitch lead the party of visitors into the compound. He noticed that James was not with them, nor was he anywhere around the area.

Garibaldi and Barnett both stood and genuflected when the NVA general approached the porch. Van Pao smiled; she wasn't sure that Spencer would obey the camp rules when senior officers visited. It had nothing to do with her; Garibaldi had explained that it was proper for them to show respect to officers senior to them. This was the first general to visit the camp, and it was the first time that Garibaldi had shown the Vietnamese sign of respect.

"Hi, soldiers!" The starlet smiled and tried acting cheerful. "What state are you from?" She spoke to Garibaldi first.

"I'm a professional soldier and we've lived all over the country." Garibaldi struggled to keep his voice calm. He recognized the woman from her roles in the movies. She was a big-name star. Garibaldi swore to himself that if he ever escaped from the camp and made it back to the States, he would never go to see one of her pictures again. "We've bought a retirement home in Colorado."

"Oh! Really? I have a small place at Aspen. . . . We're almost neighbors!" The phony statement made Garibaldi's stomach roll. He hoped that he wouldn't have to take a shit. He had little control over his bowels, and the rich food he'd been given the night before was passing right through him.

A guard approached the group and bowed to the general before placing a pot on the porch that contained a boiled chicken and vegetables.

"Mmmmm . . . that smells good!" She sniffed the pot. "At least the North Vietnamese treat you well. . . . It's better than living in a dirty foxhole somewhere . . . isn't it?" She addressed Spencer.

Lieutenant Van Pao glared at Spencer as he just stood there looking at the American woman.

"It depends on what you're *doing* in the foxhole." Spencer's voice was soft.

The manager noticed Spencer for the first time. The heat and insects were tormenting him. He had been swatting at anything that moved since he got off the helicopter. He noticed how handsome the younger soldier was, even though he was a good fifteen pounds underweight. "Soldier, how old are you?" The lisp was evident and exaggerated.

Garibaldi prayed Spencer wouldn't say something they both would regret.

"Seventeen."

"Seventeen! You're just a boy! You should be chasing *girls* down Hollywood Boulevard!" The queer manager batted his eyes at Spencer.

"I'd like to; would you mind taking me with you when you leave?" Spencer grinned.

"Mmmm . . . that sounds like fun, but I don't think our friends here would like that very much. . . . Maybe later." The man looked away shyly.

Garibaldi felt like puking.

"Where are you from?" the actress asked Spencer.

He looked directly into her eyes and then quickly down at the ground. She mistook the submissive act for shyness; actually, Spencer knew that if he continued looking at her he would punch out her capped teeth.

Spencer continued studying the ground. "The *United States of America*." The statement was complete and she didn't push it.

"Well, it was nice talking to you. I can see that you have been well cared for, but that is to be expected. The North Vietnamese are a *civilized* people. It is *we* who can learn from them. We are the aggressors!" She brushed a wisp of loose hair out of her eyes. "Is there anything you would like me to tell anyone back home?" She looked at Barnett and then at Garibaldi.

Garibaldi hesitated and then decided it was more important for his wife to know that he was still alive than to say nothing to the woman. "Yes, would you tell my wife that I'm alive . . . I'm fine. . . . My name is Salvador Garibaldi."

"Oh . . . Italian . . . I'll have to write that one down." She searched for a pen and paper. Her manager pulled out his notebook and handed it to the colonel. He wrote his name, rank, and serial number down, and then he wrote Spencer's name. He wanted someone to know that both of them were alive and were POWs.

"How about you, young man?"

Spencer shook his head.

"Come on! There must be someone back home you want me to talk to!"

Spencer shook his head again and saw that Van Pao was giving him a threatening glare. "I'm an orphan."

The statement was more of a shock to Garibaldi than it was to the celebrity. He had assumed Spencer had a family back home just like almost everyone else did. He felt embarrassed about all of the things he had told the boy about his family.

The actress turned to leave. "I'm sorry about that."

Spencer smiled. The NVA general and Lieutenant Van Pao had their backs to them and were starting toward the gate. The starlet paused and turned back to face the POWs. Her manager stopped also and smiled at Spencer.

"Have courage. The war will be over soon, and they will release you. I'm sure of that."

Spencer checked to make sure the general and Van Pao still had their backs to him and gave the movie star the finger. "Thank you so much for coming to visit us." His voice was soft but he rammed his finger at her and then at the manager.

"Oh . . . my!" She covered her mouth with the back of her hand.

Van Pao turned to see Barnett genuflecting to the actress, and she smiled. He was learning humility.

The camp staff and visitors left the small American compound and walked toward the NVA quarters. The general had never visited A Rum and requested through his staff that he be given a completed tour when he brought the famous American for a visit. A pair of North Vietnamese photographers had been taking pictures for a photo journal that would be issued worldwide, and the general wanted some shots of his soldiers and the way that they lived in the jungle while they served the Communist cause.

What happened next was a totally serendipitous result of the senior general's visit to the camp. The sergeant in charge of the guard detail had made an error on the roster and had one squad guarding the general's helicopter that should have been assigned to POW duty. The guards who had been on duty at the American compound were instructed to accompany the visitors back to their barracks and to stand by for the general's inspection. The error left both the American compound and the south side of the camp unguarded.

The old Montagnard chief saw the error almost instantly from his longhouse porch. He reacted with the speed of an old mountain warrior who had survived the jungle for over sixty years.

The nine-year-old boy ran up to the unlocked gate and pushed it open. His grandfather had told him they would have only a very few minutes head start, but that would be enough if they could reach the jungle. The boy had been instructed to lead them south for a short distance and then head *west* along the Rao Lao until they came to the first rapids, where they were to hide until some Montagnard warriors could be sent to guide them safely to the Americans in the A Shau Valley. The old chief knew the American boy couldn't make it all the way to the A Shau without help.

Garibaldi saw the boy's head in the doorway and frowned. He couldn't figure out why the small child was there at that time of day. The youth beckoned rapidly and spoke in a high-pitched voice filled with excitement. Garibaldi touched Barnett and pointed to the nine-year-old.

"It looks like he wants us to follow him." Spencer stepped over to where the boy stood and touched his shoulder and then tapped his own chest. "You want me?" Spencer pointed back at the boy, and he nodded his head vigorously. "Yes! He wants us to follow him."

Garibaldi rushed over to the door and looked out. "The guards are gone!"

The next few minutes were all reaction without much thinking. Garibaldi ran back to his cot and removed the knives. Barnett grabbed a couple of the new blankets off the beds and a set of the eating utensils. He ran after Garibaldi and the boy and followed them through the open gate into the jungle. Spencer ran with the blankets rolled up under one arm and the knife, fork, and spoon clenched in his other hand. The two American POWs were functioning off pure adrenaline and the energy the food had given them from the night before; neither of them had any idea where they were going in the jungle. They had placed their trust in a nine-year-old boy.

The narrow path they were on was used almost exclusively by Bru hunters and messengers. The NVA rarely discovered one of the Bru secret trails—and when they did, the paths looked like they led to nowhere. The boy slipped down the path like a will-o'-the-wisp and had to stop frequently for the Americans to catch up. His grandfather had told him they would be weak and tire easily. He felt no fear. His grandfather had told him to take the Americans to the first rapids, and he would obey him. The NVA meant nothing to him. He had lived his whole life with the NVA soldiers coming and going from the villages his tribe built. He did not like them, because they had hurt his grandfather, but he didn't fear them. They were like the big cobras: something always there in the jungle, simply to be avoided.

The escape to the river was easy, because it was all downhill. The boy found the river path and pointed in the direction they would take. Both Garibaldi and Spencer noticed that they were heading south, away from the South Vietnamese border. A second's worth of fear slithered down the colonel's spine. The Montagnards might be *stealing* them, for another purpose—to be used as slaves. The colonel had read Conrad's *Heart of Darkness* in college, and the idea of human slaves in the twentieth century had bothered him, especially the part where they had blinded the man so that he couldn't escape, and then they used him to grind grain.

Barnett hissed to gain the colonel's attention and gestured that he should follow the boy. Garibaldi blinked and started walking; it was too late to turn back now. He had one of the knives and decided that if the Montagnards intended on using them as slaves, he would kill himself.

The jungle was much different from how Spencer had seen it before. The animals became quiet as they passed but started their normal noise almost immediately when their backs were to them. The boy moved down the narrow path dodging and weaving, leaving hardly a leaf rustling. He carried a youth's crossbow that would kill a man at very close range but had been designed for shooting birds and small game.

Spencer heard the rapids and knew they were approaching the Rao Lao River, but he didn't know which part of the landmark they were at. The river ran from the west down the mountain range and emptied into the A Shau Valley. With the river as a guide, Spencer knew that he could find the Special Forces camp in the valley.

The boy paused and pointed up at the side of the cliff overlooking the rapids. He started up the mist-covered rocks and paused again to encourage the Americans to follow him. He smiled and waved. Garibaldi started up the cliff using the same handholds the boy had selected and carefully moved along the narrow ledge a step at a time. The boy stopped when the ledge widened and pointed at a natural cave that was hidden from view from below.

Spencer joined them. "Nice place." The lip of rock kept the majority of the mist from entering the cave, and even though it was damp inside, it was comfortable.

The boy used sign language to tell them to stay there and wait for him to return. Spencer sat down next to Garibaldi and the two of them sighed almost in unison. Spencer laughed.

"Damn, am I tired!" Spencer leaned his head back against the rock. "Here . . ." He handed Garibaldi one of the blankets.

"We've been traveling for at least three hours, maybe four." Garibaldi wrapped the blanket around his shoulders and lay down on his side. He fell into an exhausted sleep almost instantly.

Spencer curled up next to the colonel and was sleeping within a minute. He was scared, but free.

Lieutenant Van Pao was happy. The general had complimented her on the operation of A Rum and hinted that she might be promoted soon. He had been taken separately to see Mohammed James and had been very pleased with the information James was supplying to the NVA cause. He had given Van Pao the credit for James's extreme cooperation and had informed her that the American movie star's visit was worth ten North Vietnamese divisions in the field. The propaganda value of her visit was immense and would be a tremendous demoralizing factor for the American troops fighting in Vietnam.

Van Pao heard the rapid beat of a pair of Ho Chi Minh sandals slapping against the ground and the heavy breathing as the soldier reached her hooch. The sergeant stuck his head through the doorway without asking permission and ruined her day.

"The Americans have escaped!" His words cut through her like a wire whip.

"*Both* of them?"

He answered with a curt nod.

She removed her pistol and pointed it at his head and then lowered it and rushed to the door. "Find them!"

The NCO tried squeezing past her and she hit his back with the barrel, knocking him down on all fours.

"Find them or you will be fed to Mother Kaa!" The threat was a real one, and the soldier knew it.

The Montagnard boy returned with three Bru warriors from one of the dozen small Bru villages that lined the Rao Lao River. The men brought food and mats to lie on. A small warming fire was built in the safe cave, and the men spent the night there. Spencer and Garibaldi slept the sleep of the exhausted, and both of them were stiff the next morning but happy. They were free, and if their luck held out, they would be in the Special Forces camp in three or four days of walking.

The Montagnard warriors guided them almost due east along the mountain ridges, using hidden paths and jungle trails. A couple of times they heard rifle shots from NVA search parties, but they were always far to the north of them. The trip would become much more difficult once they broke out of the high mountains. There they would be forced to travel through the low hills in the A Shau Valley, where there were numerous NVA scouts and patrols.

The boy stopped frequently as they traveled to check on the condition of the Americans. He had to ask the warriors to help Garibaldi and Spencer up steep inclines. The Americans were losing their strength very fast, and the pace had to be adjusted almost every hour.

The second day of traveling after leaving the cave brought them to the source of the stream they had been using as a guiding landmark. The three warriors spoke to the boy and then shook hands with Spencer and the colonel before disappearing into the jungle.

"Do you know what's going on?" Spencer asked the colonel.

"I think they've gone as far as they're allowed to go by their village chief." Garibaldi looked around. "Let's climb to the crest and look for a landmark."

Garibaldi took the lead, with the boy bringing up the rear. He wondered how close they were to the border. The crest of the mountain was covered with thick jungle, and it was impossible to see anything unless you climbed one of the large mahogany trees. Barnett volunteered to make the climb and slipped down to the ground a couple of times before he found the right handholds in the vines that were attached to the trunk of the tree. He climbed a good fifty feet off the ground before he could see over the tops of the second-canopy trees down in the valley below them.

"Can you see anything?" Garibaldi called up in the loudest voice that he dared use.

Spencer's chest muscles tightened and pressed the air out of his lungs when he saw the Special Forces camp cut out of the tall grasses that covered the valley floor about six miles east of their location. The fog was gone and the dark greens twinkled in the bright light, contrasting against the red clay that outlined the fighting camp from the constant bulldozing of the fire lanes around the camp. It looked small from where Spencer was, but he could recall almost every single one of the bunkers and the faces of the Special Forces team. Safety was so close, yet so very far away.

"I see the SF camp down in the valley." Spencer scurried back down the vines and dropped the last ten feet—a mistake, he realized the second his feet touched the ground. They were still very tender and the long walk down the trails had opened up some of the cuts.

"How long do you think it'll take us to get there?" Garibaldi was actually accepting the idea that they just might make it to safety.

"I'd say about a half-day, maybe less if we're lucky. It's mostly downhill all the way, but the camp will be watched by the NVA, and I'd hate to almost make it there and then get killed. We'll have to be really careful the last couple thousand meters." Spencer thought a second and added, "We might be lucky enough to run into a patrol from the camp."

"We'll have to be careful about that too . . . and keep an eye on the boy. He might get shot by accident." Garibaldi placed his hand on the youth's shoulder and squeezed gently as he had seen the boy's grandfather do. He was careful not to break a Montagnard taboo, like pat the boy's head. The

Montagnards thought that a person could pat the evil spirit Tang Lie into the heads of children.

The boy smiled up at the colonel and pointed in the direction of the Special Forces camp.

"I think he has already decided on taking us there." Garibaldi smiled down at the boy. "He's been there once—to take that photograph I found to the Americans."

She growled a warning at the noise and the smell of the invaders. It was a soft, almost bored growl, but it carried along the jungle floor the hundred meters from her cave to the large mahogany tree Spencer Barnett had climbed. Garibaldi and Spencer had missed the sound, but the Montagnard boy heard it, and his reaction was almost instantaneous. There were few things in the Asian jungles that brought uncontrolled fear to a Montagnard; one of them was the growl of a hungry tiger. The boy knew instantly from her low, throaty, guttural cough that she was both irritated and hungry. He hit Barnett across his rear with the crossbow and pointed for him to get back up the tree, and then he ran over to Colonel Garibaldi and repeated the act.

Spencer paused. "What's wrong with him?"

"I think he wants us to climb the tree. . . ." Garibaldi looked at the boy, trying to understand why he was so excited all of a sudden.

The nine-year-old pushed Garibaldi against the tree and then ran over and shoved Spencer before he started climbing as fast as he could. They had been warned, and if they were stupid enough to stay on the ground—well then, he would have to tell his grandfather that they had been too stupid to help themselves and had been eaten by a tiger.

Spencer felt the boy's fear and looked around the jungle that hugged the narrow path. He felt a primeval survival shiver run along his spine. "I think we'd better just trust the kid, Colonel." Spencer started climbing up the vines. The boy had already reached the first fork in the branches and had turned back to encourage the Americans to climb faster. "Come on, sir."

The colonel stood on the jungle floor and looked up the trunk for a better avenue to the large branch the boy sat on. He could see the fear in the child's face and decided that he should just start climbing.

Spencer reached the branch and straddled it. The boy started talking rapidly in Bru and pointed down at the ground. Barnett smiled at him and then looked where the kid was pointing. She was directly under the tree, looking up at Garibaldi struggling with a loose vine. The colonel lost his grip with his left hand, and all of his weight was transferred to his right hand. He swung against the tree and dug his toes into the matting of vines to regain his balance. He fought not to fall the fifteen feet back down to the ground.

"Colonel . . . don't fall . . . *hang on!*" Spencer leaned forward on the branch with his arm held out.

"I don't think I can make it up this way; I'm going to climb back down and come up the side you did. . . ." Garibaldi looked up to where the boy and Spencer sat.

"I don't think that's a good idea, Colonel. . . ." Spencer tried keeping the fear out of his voice; he didn't want the colonel to panic.

"I can't make it up this way, Spence!"

"Look down over your shoulder and see if you change your mind. . . ."

Garibaldi flashed an angry look at Spencer and looked over his shoulder. She was *huge*. The tufts of fur sticking out around her face made her head look as large as a washtub as she studied the live meat in the tree. She had gained a few more pounds with her pregnancy, which filled out her sides a little more, but she was huge anyway.

"Oh shit . . ." Garibaldi whispered the words.

"Come on!" Spencer didn't need to encourage him again.

Suddenly Garibaldi found handholds in the vines he hadn't seen before, and he scurried up the tree with a new-found energy. He straddled the branch behind the Montagnard boy and leaned back against the trunk.

"Oh shit!" Garibaldi exhaled so hard that he could have extinguished a match twenty feet away.

Spencer had been watching the tiger circling the tree as she looked for a way up. "There's something wrong with her hip."

Garibaldi risked another look down at the beast. "It looks like a hunk of her fur has been burnt and her leg has been broken. . . ."

"Yeah . . . look how it bends out funny." Spencer looked at the colonel and added, "I wonder why she didn't just reach up the tree and swat you off the vines. . . ."

"What do you mean?" Garibaldi swallowed air down his dry throat.

"She was under you when you were only eight or ten feet off the ground. A normal tiger could have easily jumped up that high and had you."

"Shit, Spencer! You didn't need to tell me that!" Garibaldi realized how, if he had walked around the tree looking for a better way up it just *one* extra time, he would have been lunch for——he looked at the tiger's rear end as it slipped behind the tree——her.

"I haven't seen a tiger that big in a zoo." Spencer had been to only one zoo, but the tigers there had been well fed and were bigger than the ones normally found in the wild. The tigress circling the tree below them seemed to be a good two hundred, maybe three hundred pounds larger than the ones at the zoo.

Garibaldi watched her for a half-hour before he spoke. "I think she's a man-eater."

"Why do you say that?" Spencer had been watching her too.

"Look at the way she hobbles. . . . She could never catch deer and wild pigs . . . and she's way too *fat*." Garibaldi balked at his next thought. "She's probably been living off dead animals from bomb strikes. . . ."

The full force of Garibaldi's statement hit Barnett all at once. "That bitch!" Barnett pulled his eight-inch knife out of his waist string and start climbing down the trunk.

Garibaldi grabbed him and pulled him back into the fork of the tree. "Where in the hell do you think you're going!"

"That bitch *ate* Fillmore!"

Garibaldi didn't understand what Barnett was babbling, but he could see that the young soldier was very upset. "Spencer! You can't kill a tiger with a *knife*! *Now stop it!*"

Spencer leaned back against the colonel, realizing that what he had heard was true. He started crying softly. "You bitch! . . . You bitch!"

The Montagnard boy sat on the limb and watched the man cry. He wondered what was making the man cry. They were safe from the tigress in the tree; there was no reason for the man to cry.

Garibaldi waited until Spencer had gained control of himself and then he asked him about Fillmore.

Spencer shook his head. He didn't want to talk about it.

The tigress lay down next to the trunk of the tree and started licking her front paws. Her tail flicked every once in a while as she waited patiently for the meat to come down out of the tree and be eaten. Monkeys would usually panic after a few minutes and try jumping out of the tree and running to what they thought was a safer tree.

Darkness came, and she was still waiting. Garibaldi had Spencer and the boy all straddle the branch in front of him and hold on to one another. He remained closest to the trunk, with Barnett sitting in front of him holding the small Montagnard boy. The order on the branch was based on size, with the colonel being the tallest; it would have been hardest for him to balance himself farther out on the branch. All three of them knew they wouldn't fall asleep during the night, but they might doze off. A single mistake, and they would not have a second chance.

There was no moon. A heavy cloud cover had slipped in during the night and blocked out all of the light. The tigress coughed, letting everyone up in the tree know that she was still waiting. It made no difference if you closed your eyes or kept them open. The darkness was the same. The Montagnard boy scooted back against Spencer on the branch. The darkness and the hated man-eater were scaring him. Spencer placed both of his arms over the boy's shoulders and hugged him against his chest. He heard the child sigh, and then the tiny boy dropped his head against Spencer's arm and fell asleep.

"You awake, Colonel?"

"There's no way I'm going to fall asleep with her down there!" Garibaldi whispered into Spencer's ear. "I'm not Tarzan!"

Spencer smiled in the dark. The colonel had a sense of humor. "Fillmore was on patrol with us, and the night before we ran into the NVA ambush he was pulled out of his fox-hole by a tiger and hauled off into the jungle screaming for help. . . . Man! That was some heavy shit. . . ." Spencer stopped talking long enough to catch his breath. "You know, I had forgotten all about that until she came along." Barnett looked down but couldn't see the tigress lying on the ground below them.

"That's pretty normal . . . most people block stuff like that out of their minds." Garibaldi reached up and squeezed Spencer's shoulder. "It must have been pretty bad having to listen to all that. . . ."

"You can't imagine!" Spencer shook his head from side to side. "It was horrible, listening to his screams fading away in the jungle and there wasn't a fucking thing we could do!" The Montagnard boy jerked in his sleep and Spencer squeezed him. "What I'd give for a fucking gun right now! With just *one* fucking bullet!"

"At least she didn't get one of us, Spence." Garibaldi adjusted his position on the branch. "You've got to look for the good things, or you'll go crazy."

"Colonel . . . I think I'm already crazy." Spencer spoke the sentence matter-of-factly, without having to accent it.

Garibaldi nodded his head in agreement, but the darkness hid the gesture. "Me too . . ."

The first rays of morning light let the tree dwellers know that the big cat was still with them. She had slept the whole night under the tree. She could smell the fresh meat above her head and roared her anger and her hunger. The sound traveled for miles in the quiet jungle. She roared again, ending it in a snarl.

"I think she's pissed." Spencer spit, trying to hit her. "Hey, bitch! You hungry?" He spat again, and it landed right on the tip of her nose.

She roared and shook her head from side to side, trying to dislodge the horrible man-smell from her sensory organ.

"You don't like that, bitch?" Spencer almost laughed.

The Montagnard boy looked at Spencer with an expression of total respect. He was taken in by Spencer's bravery.

"This is getting to be a bit too much." Garibaldi tried adjusting his position on the branch, but nothing worked after the all-night vigil. "Maybe she'll leave if she gets hungry enough."

"I'm more worried about the NVA finding us right now than her. . . . She can't stay down there much longer."

"So what if she leaves. . . . I don't really relish the idea of getting down from here and trying to make it to the A Shau camp with her nearby."

"We really don't have much of a choice." Spencer didn't like the idea either. There was one good thought, though: they would have no problem wanting to take breaks on their way.

The NVA patrol heard the tiger roar. It was the first time any of the city-raised soldiers had heard that sound in the wild. The sergeant pushed the safety off his AK-47 and dropped down into a battle-ready squat, turning slowly from side to side. The parachute cloth he used for a camouflage cape ruffled in the breeze, coming down the mountain trail. He signaled for the point man to continue down the mountain trail in the direction they had been going, directly toward the roar.

She coughed and moved her head from side to side with her mouth open in a quiet snarl. The smell was too strong coming down the trail. She looked up at the meat in the tree and snarled again before leaving to find something better to eat.

"I think she's leaving!" Barnett took a deep breath, hoping that she wouldn't turn around and come back at the sound of his voice. She slipped off the trail into the thick brush.

"We'd better wait a while before getting down. She might be trying to trick us." Garibaldi had reason to be paranoid.

"Fuck! She's going the same way we are. . . ." Spencer didn't like that one bit.

They waited up in the tree for an hour before deciding to get down. Spencer wouldn't let the Montagnard boy go down first and made Garibaldi hold him so that he wouldn't follow. Spence didn't enjoy the climb down one bit and stopped when he was about ten feet off the ground and waited, just in case she was lying out of sight in the brush. His hands started hurting and his grip was slipping on the vines, forcing him to finish the climb down. He felt his foot touch the ground and turned around quickly, fully expecting to see a charging tiger coming after him. What he saw instead was an NVA soldier step back onto the trail, pointing a AK-47 at his chest.

"We've got visitors, Colonel. . . ." Spencer's voice reached the colonel at the same time as the sound of a rifle butt striking flesh reached him. Spencer folded over, holding his stomach with both hands.

The NVA sergeant screamed for the colonel and the boy to come down out of the tree. Garibaldi was five feet off the ground when he felt rough hands yank him the rest of the way down.

The walk back to A Rum seemed like it would last forever. The NVA didn't spare the nine-year-old and beat him as much as they beat the Americans. Spencer didn't think he would make it. Frankly, he didn't care.

Enough was enough.

One of the NVA struck out with his rifle butt at the Montagnard boy and caught him on the side of his knee. Spencer heard the bone crack under the blow. The boy fell down on the trail, wriggling in pain, but not a sound came out of his mouth. The NVA soldier raised his rifle to shoot the boy, and Spencer stepped over and pushed it to one side. With his eyes he dared the NVA to shoot him and then reached down and swung the small-framed boy onto his back. He grabbed hold under each of the child's thighs and started walking again on the trail. The boy grabbed hold around Spencer's neck and laid his head on the soldier's back. Spencer could hear the boy whimpering softly.

Spencer had a new reason to live. He would get the boy back to his grandfather.

Lieutenant Van Pao sat on the porch of her hooch and tapped her bamboo whip against her pants leg. She had been informed by radio that the Americans had been found and that they would be arriving in camp very soon. She felt the fire for revenge burning in her throat. Everything had changed in the four days that they had been gone. She was now considered the worst POW camp commander in the North Vietnamese Army. She was told that an American had *never* escaped from one of their camps before. She was disgraced.

The guards calling back and forth alerted her that they were arriving with the POWs. She left the shade and stepped out into the clearing where she could see. Colonel Garibaldi was the first one to appear behind the camouflaged field soldier. Spencer Barnett stepped out of the jungle with the Montagnard boy on his back. She felt the hate erupt. How could they be so stupid as to let the American return a *hero* in front of the Montagnards! The NVA sergeant stopped the patrol and pulled the boy off Spencer's back. The child fell to the ground and remained there, moaning.

The Montagnard chief watched his grandson. Only a person experienced in the ways of the mountain people would have noticed that the old man was very disturbed. He kept a poker face as he walked over to where his grandson lay. One of the field soldiers pushed the old man back away from the boy, using his rifle.

"What you two have done will cost you a great deal! *One*

of you will die a very slow, painful death . . . while the other one watches!" Van Pao hissed out the words. "Tonight you will have time to think about it and wonder which one of you will be so *lucky* as to die!" She whirled and walked away.

The POW camp sergeant screamed orders to his men, who grabbed Spencer and Garibaldi and dragged them back to their old cages. One of the guards grabbed the boy by his broken leg, and the youth released a high-pitched scream, then caught himself and bit his tongue.

Lieutenant Van Pao stopped walking and turned around with an evil smile on her face. She barked out some orders to her guard, and he picked up the boy and carried him into her hut.

Barnett and Garibaldi had both been beaten by the NVA sergeant who had made the mistake with the guard roster and had allowed for their escape. The Americans spent the night lying on the floors of their stripped cages. Their exhausted state from the escape and the all-night vigil allowed them to pass out and sleep most of the night.

A guard woke Barnett by pulling him out of the cage onto the ground, and then the pain from the guard's heel in his side brought Spencer to his feet. Garibaldi was already standing next to Mother Kaa's cage, waiting for Spencer. The look in the colonel's eyes told Spencer that the old officer was near the point of giving up.

Spencer knew that if he said anything he would be beaten, but he risked it anyway. He looked directly at Garibaldi and spoke. "You chickenshit fucking *officer*! Don't you have any fucking guts?" Spencer butted the colonel with his shoulder. "At least think of your wife and kids! Live for *them*!"

Garibaldi blinked and came out of his mental coma of self-pity to see Spencer fall to the ground from the rabbit punch.

Lieutenant Van Pao, Mohammed James, and all of the Montagnard villagers were standing in a semicircle facing the jungle when Garibaldi and Barnett arrived with their guards. Spencer saw the nine-year-old Montagnard boy who had helped them escape sitting on the ground with his legs tied Indian fashion. The guards had used nylon cord to tie the boy's calves up against his thighs. The pain from his broken leg must have been excruciating. The boy's hands had been tied behind his back, and then a nylon cord had been wrapped tightly around his upper arms to hold them against his sides. The boy was naked.

"I want you to see what happens to enemies of the People's Republic of North Vietnam!" She nodded her head and two of the camp guards picked up the small boy by grabbing his bound thighs and arms.

Spencer couldn't figure out what they were going to do with the kid.

Garibaldi let out a soft cry and then started begging Van Pao. "Please . . . please . . . spare the boy. . . . He's just a kid!"

Van Pao smiled. "Would you like to take his place, Colonel?"

Garibaldi looked down at the ground in shame.

Spencer looked from Garibaldi to Van Pao and then over to James, trying to figure out what was going on, and then his eyes rested on the clump of bamboo growing at the edge of the clearing. One of the two-inch-thick poles had been cut off about three feet above the ground, and the end had been sharpened to a needle point.

Barnett understood what they were going to do to the boy.

"Van Pao!" Spencer tried taking a step toward her but was restrained by the guards on each side of him. "Let the boy go, and I'll tell you everything I know . . . *everything!*"

The lieutenant smiled at Barnett, then the look changed to one of pure hate. "You are too late, Spencer Barnett! Some of your friends returned and destroyed the sensors!" She spat at him. "You have nothing that I want!" She looked at the guards holding the boy and nodded her head. They lifted him up and held him over the sharpened stake. Some of the Montagnard women started to wail.

"Wait!" Spencer struggled against his guards. *"I'll* take his place!"

She turned around slowly, smiling a full-mouthed grin. "Fine!"

James looked over at Barnett with an expression of total disbelief on his face. "You fool! He's just an ignorant Montagnard! He's not worth it!"

Spencer looked over at James and smiled, using only the right side of his mouth. "Would he be worth it if he was *black*?"

The sound of the slap across Spencer's face echoed through the village. "You white motherfucker!"

Van Pao stopped James from hitting Barnett again. She gave her guards orders to prepare the American for the bamboo stake. They stripped him naked in front of the assembled villagers and bound him in exactly the same fashion as they had tied the boy.

Garibaldi watched as they wound the nylon parachute cord around Spencer's upper body. He bit his lip and swore to himself that if he survived the POW camp, he was going to submit the young soldier for the Medal of Honor.

Van Pao waited until her guards were finished tying Spencer, then she lit up a Salem cigarette—she had changed her brand to something a little stronger—and looked over at Garibaldi. "Would you like to take *his* place?" She nodded at Spencer.

Colonel Garibaldi dropped his head in shame.

"Come on, Colonel! *You're* the leader . . . are you going to let your soldier die?"

Colonel Garibaldi's lower lip trembled. He was so ashamed, but he didn't have the courage to take Spencer Barnett's place.

"Well, answer me!" Van Pao screamed at the colonel.

Garibaldi kept looking down at the ground and whispered, "No."

Spencer saw what the NVA lieutenant was doing. She was going to kill him, but at the same time she was going to totally break the colonel and turn him into a mental case.

"Hey! Sweet Bitch! I won't *let* him take my place!" Barnett screamed over at the colonel, "Damn you, sir! Don't you fall for this shit! You know the game she's playing!"

One of the guards kicked Spencer in the side to shut him up, and he yelled all the louder.

"Colonel! You've got to live for *both* of us!"

Garibaldi's head snapped up, and he looked directly at Spencer. "You bet your ass on that one, Spencer Barnett!"

Spencer smiled.

Lieutenant Van Pao curled her lip. "You stupid, stupid . . . fool." She barked orders to the guards, and they picked Spencer up by his thighs, one guard on each side. A third guard held his hands against the soldier's back to balance him. They placed him directly over the sharpened stake and lowered him until his rectum touched the very tip of the bamboo rod that was still anchored in the ground by its own root system.

Spencer felt the point of the stake enter his rectal passage about an inch and then a sharp pain when the point scraped against the wall of his colon. He clenched his jaws.

"Does it hurt, Spencer Barnett?" Van Pao smiled and flipped her cigarette at the soldier. The butt struck his chest, sending a spray of red coals over his bare flesh. Spencer glared at the woman. He was terrified, but there was no way he would give her or James the pleasure of knowing that he was. He concentrated on a short prayer, asking Jesus Christ to let him die swiftly.

"Don't close your eyes, Spencer . . . I want to see those baby blues." James took a step forward but was stopped by Van Pao. She shook her head.

The Montagnard chief watched along with the rest of his villagers. They did not need an interpreter to tell them that the American had volunteered to replace the boy on the stake. One of the village elders started beating on the gong he had carried with him to the assembly. The solitary musical instrument made the only sound in the whole village; even the animals sensed that it was best to remain quiet.

Van Pao pointed at the boy and barked orders rapidly in

Vietnamese. The guards lowered their weapons and pointed them at the villagers. A heavy 12.7mm machine gun had been rolled out on its small wheels and set up facing the group.

The guards removed Spencer from the stake. They had not lowered him far enough to draw blood, but Spencer had been made aware of what could have happened to him. The guards picked up the nine-year-old and lowered him down on the stake. They did not stop. The boy screamed when the stake tore into his intestines. Spencer had been placed four feet in front of the stake, facing the child. One of the Montagnard warriors took a step forward and was shot. He fell to the ground and twitched a couple of times before he died. The pain was uncontrollable for the boy, and he screamed his nine-year-old lungs out. Spencer tried closing his eyes, but the child's face remained there under his lids, etched by emotion.

The Montagnard chief started chanting in Bru. It sounded like he was singing one of their spirit songs, but what the old man was doing was cursing the North Vietnamese and pledging a blood feud. The villagers took turns answering the old man and pledging themselves and their offspring until there would be no one left to carry on the battle with the NVA. It was extremely unusual, but even the women made the pledge. Lieutenant Van Pao should have learned the Bru language. She would have saved her country thousands of soldiers' lives, because with the single execution of the boy she had turned four hundred Bru into fanatics.

Spencer couldn't take the boy's screams anymore. He started praying out loud, begging that the boy would die quickly, before he went insane watching the cruel execution of the child.

The NVA guards forced the Bru back to their village and took Garibaldi back to his cage. Spencer Barnett was left alone, tied up and sitting four feet in front of the boy impaled on the stake. One of the guards showed a sign of mercy and placed both of his hands on the youth's shoulders and shoved down hard. The sharp bamboo stake tore through the child's chest cavity and stopped when his rear pressed against the ground. The stake had penetrated all the way to the boy's throat cavity.

The Montagnard boy's eyes bulged and his mouth opened to allow the blood to gush out. The child died with a soft rush of air coming out of his lungs.

Spencer was left sitting in front of the child all night long. He kept his eyes closed and struggled to keep his sanity.

The Bru chief instructed his elders, and during the night the whole Bru village disappeared; animals, belongings, everything except the longhouses was gone when the sun came up the next morning. Lieutenant Van Pao would start receiving reports of missing NVA soldiers and messengers before the sun rose again the next day. It would be a couple of weeks before she realized the full impact of her deed.

Spencer felt the sun against his face but refused to open his eyes. He could hear the flies landing on and taking off from the small body in front of him. He continued to struggle with his mind. He must live for *revenge*.

The sun was almost directly overhead when a pair of guards came and cut his legs free. He couldn't stand up, and the rush of blood to his starved legs caused a terrible pain. Spencer kept his eyes tightly shut until he had been thrown back in his cage.

"Spencer, I'm sorry. . . ." Garibaldi tried saying more, but the words just wouldn't come out.

CHAPTER SEVEN

Philippine Mock-up

The C-141 Starlifter was waiting on the special restricted runway with its engines running. The two black step-vans pulled up to the jet aircraft, and McDonald's prisoner snatch team ran into the rear of the large cargo plane. A well-trained crew helped the reconnaissance men into their seats after stacking their gear on a pallet and strapping all of it down.

Brigadier General Seacourt sat inside of the command communications pod that had been loaded onto the aircraft earlier. He sipped a cup of black coffee and listened to the radio traffic coming in from the high-flying spy aircraft soaring over the target area in Laos. He felt the plane move to the end of the runway for takeoff and looked at his watch; they were right on schedule. He fastened his seatbelt and leaned his head back against the headrest on his leather swivel chair. A lever next to his seat locked the chair in place for takeoffs and landings.

Woods looked around the dark aircraft and saw the olive-drab communications pod and another one of the portable containers strapped down on the roller bearings that were used to slide heavy cargo to the back of the aircraft. David had been surprised when the vans pulled up to the Starlifter instead of to helicopters. He was puzzled, along with the rest of the team—except for Master Sergeant McDonald, who knew that they were flying to the island of Palawan in the Philippine archipelago.

The Air Force crew served the team hot dinners from the food warmers that had been brought on board, and beer and wine were served with the meal. Woods listened to rock music over the headsets in the lounge chair he occupied. Two pallets of specially designed first-class seats had been loaded aboard the Starlifter for the flight, and all of the team relaxed in the luxury.

The three Bru recon team members toyed with their food and laughed when Sergeant Cooper and Lieutenant Nappa showed them how the headsets worked. The Montagnards pulled the headsets off their ears each time one of the Special Forces men put them on the tribesmen.

McDonald checked to make sure all of his men were taken care of and opened the door to the communications pod where the general was waiting for him.

"Hello, Sergeant." Seacourt held out his hand. "I want to congratulate you on an excellent team prep. . . . They really look good."

"Thanks, General . . . but you're too early on the congratulations. When we bring *out* the POWs will be the time for celebrating."

"I think you've done an excellent job, regardless . . . we can't control the luck factor." Seacourt sipped his coffee, and then realizing that he was using bad manners, added, "Would you like a cup?"

"I'd love one, General. That's my biggest vice . . . coffee." McDonald took a seat at the same time. "What's the intelligence on A Rum?"

"There's been quite a bit of traffic lately. It seems that the Montagnards have pulled out of the village lock, stock, and barrel." Seacourt frowned. "G-2 doesn't know what to make of it."

"It's not a warning that they're going to switch camps . . . is it?" McDonald felt his stomach turn. He didn't want to lose Barnett now that they were so close to freeing him.

"We don't know, but we're not taking any chances." Seacourt tapped the edge of the table with the fingers on his free hand. "We've cut your Philippine trip back to *one* day."

McDonald nodded in agreement. The training would have been perfect, but it wouldn't be worth shit if the NVA moved the POWs.

The general and the sergeant listened to the incoming radio traffic for a few minutes, then the general slapped his leg and smiled. "I almost forgot! If you want to make a telephone call home to your wife, go ahead and use the airborne tele-link system. We've got a couple of hours to kill."

McDonald looked down into his coffee. "Thanks, General . . . but I don't have anyone to call. . . . Do you mind if I let the men use the system?"

"Sure! Go ahead!" Seacourt felt his face turn a little red. He didn't know why, but he felt that he had said the wrong thing to McDonald.

Seacourt moved to the second command pod and gave the men a little privacy for their calls home. The tele-link was a regular AT&T airborne hookup, so the men had the normal privacy and clarity of a telephone call. McDonald had allotted ten minutes per person and had instructed each of them that they were not allowed to talk about the mission or where they were calling from, except that they were still in Vietnam. The rest of their conversations was their business.

Arnason passed on making a call back to the States. He sat in the wide luxury seat and chain-smoked. The small ashtray in the arm of the chair was full, and he used a paper coffeecup to flick his ashes in. McDonald sat next to Arnason. It was ironic that both of the American warriors had lost their families, one through a tragic accident and the other through a tragic divorce.

McDonald let his thoughts wander back to the past. He recalled how his son would climb trees when he was four years old and jump down to him from the limbs. The boy had total trust in him. McDonald smiled. He was remembering the day he had been cutting his lawn and a neighbor stopped by to borrow a sander. He had taken a break and they were both drinking a beer and walking around his front lawn talking about the best way to grow grass. He had heard a voice in the back of his mind but had ignored it. The next thing he saw was a small body falling down from the tree he was standing next to. He dropped his beer and tried catching him, but it was too late. His son landed on the grass at his feet. McDonald caught himself breathing hard again as he sat in the aircraft recalling the incident. He thought his son had broken his neck, but the boy shook his head and struggled to his feet and gave him a look that he would never forget, followed by, "You were supposed to *catch* me, Dad!" That had been the first and last time that he had ever let the boy down.

"Whatever you're thinking about must be pretty good." Arnason leaned over and spoke to McDonald. "You're smiling like a Cheshire cat."

McDonald nodded his head. "You're right . . . it is pretty good. Aren't you going to call home?"

"Naw . . . There's nothing back there for me. . . . I had a bad divorce."

"That seems to be going around a lot lately." McDonald looked over and saw the last man enter the communications pod for his call back home. He checked his watch and saw that they had about half an hour before arriving at the military airstrip on Palawan.

Woods picked up the regular telephone and looked down at the touch-tone numbers. He blinked his eyes trying to recall his area code back home and his telephone number. He started to panic and then remembered the numbers. There was a short pause as the linkup was made, and then he heard a telephone ringing on the other end.

"Hello?" It was his dad's voice.

"Hi, Dad . . ."

A long pause filled the airwaves. "David?"

"Yep."

"David! Where are you?"

"Still in Vietnam. We have a special telephone hookup

here, and the sergeant said I could make a short call. . . . How you doing back there in America's heartland?"

"It's cold . . . we had some snow . . . but I'm doing well . . . just closed a big insurance deal, so your brother can stay in med school another year." His father was rambling, but David loved it. Just hearing his comforting voice had a calming effect. "Oh, your mother is going to die when she finds out you called! She's at the post office. . . . She's working a lot of overtime . . . but that will be good for Christmas . . . more presents for you kids." He swallowed hard and stopped rambling. "How are you doing, Davey? Are you safe?"

"Sure, Pops! I've got a lot of rear-area duty. . . . Some time in the field, but we've got super NCOs and officers in the Cav!"

"I'm glad to hear that. . . . Your mother goes to Mass every day and prays for you, son."

David nodded his head and felt the tears rolling down his cheeks. He fought hard not to let his voice break. "Tell her thanks. . . ."

"I saw one of your old professors from Lincoln Community College and he asked about you. He said that he's looking forward to your coming back. . . . You were one of his best students. . . . I forgot his name." The middle-aged man fought back the tears. He didn't want his son to know that he was going to cry.

"Yeah, I'll probably do that, Dad. . . . When I get back . . . Maybe I'll go to Georgetown and be on the same campus as Skip. . . ."

"You *will not*!" The tears rolled down his cheeks and he fought to hide the emotion in his voice. The last thing he needed was to let David know that he was crying. "I can't afford to have *two* sons going there!" He tried to laugh. David knew that his father would work sweeping the streets to send him to Georgetown if he wanted to go there.

"Well, Pops . . . I've got to go. . . . There are other guys waiting to make a call."

"So soon?"

"Yeah . . ." Woods wiped his eyes with the back of his hand. "Tell Mom that I love her. . . ."

"We love you too, son . . . a lot."

"I know . . . Gotta go. Love you, Dad." David hung up the phone.

The middle-aged man dropped down in the chair next to the telephone and wept openly. He held his head in both hands. Now that his son had hung up, there were a million *important* things he wanted to tell him. He couldn't believe that he had wasted the call by telling him such dumb things! He picked up the telephone and dialed his wife's number at work.

The C-141 Starlifter banked over the long, pencil-shaped island and lowered its landing gear. All of the team members sat in their seats facing the rear of the aircraft. Woods could feel the wheels touch down and the engines roar as they helped brake the huge jet.

McDonald was the first one off, and he directed the team onto a military bus that had been provided for them by the Philippine Army. The ride to the secret training area was less than an hour from the airbase. Woods watched the scenery as they drove down the hard-packed dirt road and noticed that there was little difference between the Philippine jungle and that of Vietnam. The bus stopped and turned into a military-controlled area that had guards at the gates. The bus was searched by a Filipino lieutenant and two soldiers and then was allowed to enter. Woods looked over at Sergeant McDonald, who remained sitting at the front of the bus, smoking casually.

Kirkpatrick leaned over and whispered to Woods, "Do you know what the fuck is going on?"

Woods shook his head in the negative and shrugged his shoulders. "We'll find out soon enough."

The bus pulled up to an open area and stopped. McDonald stood and turned to face the team sitting on the light green seats. "We're only going to be here for the day. We'll be flying back tonight. We had planned on having three days here for training, but things are beginning to deteriorate, and we are going to have to move fast or not at all."

"They haven't moved the POWs, have they?" Lieutenant Nappa from CCN asked the question.

McDonald frowned. "To be honest, we don't know. . . ."

"Let's go!" Woods picked up his gear and started leaving the bus. "Let's not waste any time."

McDonald led the team over to where General Seacourt sat waiting under a thatched open-air cabana. The men lined their gear up along the back of the classroom and took seats on the logs that had been provided for that purpose.

"I know that we've kept you in the dark so far." Seacourt stood with his hands on his hips and his thumbs hooked around his black leather pistol belt. "So now's the time to clear up any questions you might have." He walked over to a large blackboard with buildings drawn on it. "This is an exact replica of a village in Laos called A Rum." He pointed to the drawings and then stepped back so that the team would have an unrestricted view of the buildings that occupied the clearing behind the general. "And that is an exact mock-up of the village and what we think are POW long-houses. . . ." He pointed.

Woods was very impressed. They had made an exact, life-sized replica of the POW camp in the Philippines!

"I am not going to waste any more of your time . . . it's precious right now. We've cut your training time drastically, and you need to run through the actual assault at least a couple of times before we fly back to Vietnam." Seacourt looked at the team leader. "Master Sergeant McDonald . . . let's get on with it!"

The Philippine Army had provided assault and transport Hueys for the training, and the team had practiced their landing and assaults on the mock-up for over six hours straight without taking a break. None of the men wanted to stop until the mission had been executed perfectly. McDonald had even thrown in a couple of examples of the unexpected in the training by moving the POWs from the longhouses to locations in the surrounding jungle. He had missed nothing in the training, and they practiced the assaults and then the different methods of searching for the POWs—first through the buildings in the village and then by cloverleafing around the village from the jungle in two-man teams, with a small force acting as a reserve force. All of them had the new URC-10 hand-held radios that made communicating easy and control superb.

McDonald called for a break, and the men dropped down near exhaustion under the shade of a banana grove. Woods sipped from his canteen of water and lay back against his rucksack. Everyone had been giving a hundred percent and was feeling good. They were a *team* and were beginning to sense how one another operated.

"Woods . . . don't forget when you're going around the edge of a hut to go in low first and *then* stand up. Any NVA waiting for you will fire about chest high and won't be expecting you to look around the corner of the building from the ground."

Woods nodded.

"Kirkpatrick . . . full automatic on your CAR-15 . . . we're going to need a lot of firepower."

Kirkpatrick nodded.

"Lieutenant Reed . . . more aggressive—we can't hold back at all." McDonald remembered the cutthroats. "If we hesitate for even a minute, they'll kill the POWs before they'll let us rescue them . . . that's why we can't *hesitate*! We leave the choppers running and we don't stop until we find the POWs!"

Reed nodded.

"And . . . we will not take any prisoners—*none*. We don't have time to mess with them." McDonald didn't like that part of the mission, but they weren't equipped to take prisoners and there just wasn't enough time to tie up even one man.

McDonald struggled to his feet. "One more time, and then we head back to the plane."

* * *

Brigadier General Seacourt sat in the command pod deep in thought. He looked weird sitting in the dark with only the red lights from the radios illuminating the pod. The last radio message from his intelligence people had him worried. The door opened and McDonald stepped into the dark chamber.

"I'm glad you're awake." Seacourt offered the sergeant a seat next to him.

"Something wrong, General?"

"I've just received a message that affects our mission in a serious way." Seacourt's fingers drummed the top of the table next to him as he talked. "A group of about fifty Bru Montagnards arrived at the A Shau Special Forces camp yesterday and volunteered for duty as camp commandos. The story they brought with them involves two American POWs being held at A Rum."

"Two for sure?" McDonald wanted to confirm that Barnett was still there.

"Two POWs and a third American who is an *NVA soldier*." Seacourt lowered his head and looked at the sergeant over the rims of his glasses.

"James?"

Seacourt nodded his head in agreement. "We want him, too."

McDonald leaned back in his chair. "Dead or alive?"

"Dead or alive . . ." Seacourt stopped tapping the top of the table with his fingers.

CHAPTER EIGHT

Hero, Traitor, Deathmaker

The reports coming in from the whole district as far away as the village of Tala to the west were a disaster. NVA soldiers were being ambushed and killed by Montagnards. Their weapons were being taken and used to kill more NVA soldiers. All of the bodies had been found impaled on bamboo stakes.

Lieutenant Van Pao paced back and forth in her small office. The general was furious with her and had ordered the division's intelligence officer to replace her and move the POW camp to a new location. All that had been because of the American POWs' escape, along with the new deaths of the NVA soldiers. Van Pao was now afraid for her life. She couldn't get his name out of her thoughts: *Spencer Barnett*. He was the cause of all her problems.

Mohammed James entered her office without asking permission and took a seat in one of the bamboo chairs. "You look worried, Lieutenant."

"Shut up!"

"I think you're reading too much into what has happened. . . . Kill a few Montagnards and the rest will come back in line." James puckered his lips, and a vicious gleam filtered through his eyes. "Or you could make an example

149

out of Spencer Barnett that the Montagnards would never forget."

"Like what? We tried making an example out of that damned boy, and look where it's gotten me!" She looked out the open window over to the clump of bamboo where the nine-year-old boy's body was still impaled on the bamboo stake. The body, swollen so badly that it was unrecognizable, was covered with a mass of moving bot flies.

"Let me have him. . . ." James took a deep breath. "I guarantee that the Montagnard rebels will hear his screams ten miles away in the jungle."

"You guarantee?"

James nodded his head slowly. "Guaranteed!"

Spencer sat in his cage in a catatonic stupor. He stared out at nothing and tried not to blink his eyes. Each time his eyelids shut he could see the little boy's face. He tried not to listen because the child's screams still echoed in his ears. He tried not to smell—especially not to smell.

Colonel Garibaldi tried talking to Barnett, but the soldier heard nothing he said. The trauma with the Montagnard boy had been too much for the seventeen-year-old; it had been too much for the colonel. He reached over and touched the base of the cross he still had attached to the corner of his cage and whispered, "Help him, Lord. . . . Take the boy's burden . . . please."

Spencer blinked and looked over at the colonel. "We've got to bury him."

The colonel heard the young soldier's voice for the first time in days and closed his eyes in silent thanks.

"We'll find a way." Garibaldi eased out the words. "We'll find a way, Spence."

"Guard! *Guard!*" Barnett called the POW guard on duty over to his cage. "*Trung-uy* Van Pao . . ." The guard understood and went back to his thatch-covered guard shack and called the lieutenant on the field telephone.

James came over with the woman to Spencer's cage. He wore a brown leather pistol belt and carried a Russian 9mm pistol in a matching holster. He was dressed in a clean NVA uniform and had actually gained five pounds since he had been taken prisoner with Barnett.

"What do you want, Spencer Barnett?" Van Pao hated him more than anything she had ever hated before.

"I would like to bury the Montagnard boy." Barnett spoke through badly bruised lips.

"Fuck you, Spencer Barnett!" Van Pao screamed. "I would like to bury *you!*"

James grabbed her arm and leaned over to whisper in her ear. She smiled and then threw her head back and laughed. "Yes! *Yes!*" She gave the guard orders, and he ran to open Spencer's cage. Van Pao leaned her forehead against the cold bamboo of Barnett's cage and smiled in at him. "You can dig his grave and bury him . . . but make the hole big enough for *two!*"

The guard pulled Spencer out of his cage so hard he lost his balance and fell backward on the ground. He got back up on his feet and kicked Spencer twice.

James walked Spencer over to where the Montagnard boy was sitting upright on the bamboo shaft and shoved him down on his knees in front of the swollen body. "Damn! The fucking smell!" James pinched his nose shut and moved up-wind.

Van Pao and two of the camp guards joined them a few minutes later with a length of light chain that they wrapped around Spencer's neck and secured with a small lock. The loose end of the chain was wrapped around a six-inch bamboo stalk and secured.

Van Pao pointed to the guard carrying a small NVA field shovel, and he gave it to Spencer. "Now start digging a grave for that thing . . ." she nodded at the bloated body with her head, "and for you!"

Spencer glared at her and then over at James.

"Dig!" James tried kicking Barnett, but the soldier was a little out of range.

The small shovel was difficult to dig with in the hard-packed soil, but Spencer struggled until he broke through the top layer of red clay. He was determined to bury the boy who had been so kind to him and had shown such bravery. It would be Spencer's last project on earth, but it would be worth it to keep the flies off the boy's body.

Spencer worked hard through the whole day and had a hole dug five feet deep and about four feet long. When he stopped digging, he didn't have the strength to pull himself out of the hole, and the NVA guards had to help him.

James returned to inspect Barnett's work. He looked down in the small pit and smiled. "It's going to be a tight fit for two. . . ."

"It'll do fine. . . ." Spencer croaked the words out through dry vocal cords.

"You thirsty?"

Spencer nodded his head.

"Why didn't you tell me!" James removed a bottle of Johnny Walker Black from his nearby rucksack and handed it to Spencer.

"Water." Spencer pushed the bottle of scotch back at James.

"This or nothing!" James pushed the bottle against Spencer's chest.

"Nothing." Spencer dropped down on his knees, exhausted.

"You motherfucker!" James pushed Spencer down on his back and held him there using one of his knees while he unscrewed the top of the bottle. He poured the scotch over Spencer's face and then forced open the POW's mouth using the open end of the bottle as a lever. The scotch burned Spencer's dry throat and split lips.

"I'm going to kill you. . . ." Spencer croaked out the words.

James slapped Barnett's face. "You ain't going to kill a fucking *fly* . . . soldier boy!" He glared at the soldier, who didn't have enough strength left even to stand up. James hated him. Where did Spencer Barnett get his willpower? How could he stand up to the torture and the suffering? He was supposed to have been broken under torture a dozen times, but each time Barnett survived and flaunted his strength at him! "Bury the fucking Montagnard!"

"I need something to wrap him in. . . ." Spencer struggled to his feet.

"Throw him in the fucking hole like he is!" James drained what was left in the bottle.

"I want to wrap him up in something!" Spencer had nothing to lose. He knew that James was going to kill him, but if they wanted the boy's body taken off the stake, they were going to have to provide a burial cloth for him.

James kicked some of the dirt back into the hole and watched it shatter apart when it hit. "All right! Use *your* blanket!"

Spencer nodded and started walking back to his cage. It was pathetic the way the seventeen-year-old struggled to remain on his feet. It took him as much determination to walk the hundred meters as it would have taken a healthy person to run the Boston Marathon. Spencer made it to his cage and pulled his worn blanket out of his prison cell.

Colonel Garibaldi watched the heroic struggle and cried openly. He knew that they were going to kill the boy when he was finished digging the grave, and there was nothing he could do to prevent it.

Spencer stopped and stared into Garibaldi's cage on his way back. The guard's rifle butt failed to get him to move until he was ready, and then he started a slow shuffle back to the hole.

James had replaced the first bottle of scotch with a second one while Spencer had gone to get his blanket. "Now—bury him!"

The Montagnard boy's body was so bloated from sitting in the sun for three days that Spencer could not recognize it as his friend. The smell was horrible, and when Barnett touched the dead boy's arm a sickening gas hissed out of the body. Spencer gagged but didn't stop. He was going to bury the boy.

No one saw the Montagnard man watching from the edge of the jungle. He was so well camouflaged that you could pass by him within a few feet and still not see him. He watched the young American struggle with his son's body and remained motionless. He had been waiting for three days for a chance to sneak the body out of the camp.

Spencer wrapped the decomposing body in his blanket and dragged it to the edge of the hole. He didn't have the strength to lower it in and looked over at James for help.

"Fuck you! I ain't touching that stinking thing!" James shook his head and then tilted it back to drink.

Barnett used his feet to push the boy over the edge of the hole. The blanket held the corpse together, but when it hit the bottom, all of the gas in the boy's intestines was forced out. The smell was awful. Spencer started pushing the red clay over the boy's body, at the same time reciting the only prayer he knew, The Lord's Prayer.

"You getting fucking holy on me?" James laughed the words out.

Barnett ignored him.

"Don't put too much dirt in there. . . . You have to leave some room for you!" James staggered to his feet and looked down in the hole. *"Stop!"* He held both arms straight out like an umpire would do declaring a base runner safe. "Set down in there on top of that dirt!" He pointed into the partially filled hole.

Spencer dropped down in the grave. He was too tired to resist anymore. He was hoping James would kill him; at least all the hurting would stop. Spencer sat down Indian style on the soft dirt mound at the bottom of the grave. He could feel the earth pack down under him.

"Well . . . well . . . well! You've *finally* decided to start cooperating with us! Well, it's too fucking late!" James removed his Russian 9mm pistol from its holster and pressed the barrel hard against Spencer's forehead. "Do you have any last words?"

"Fuck you . . . James."

James laughed and moved his hand a couple of inches to the left of Barnett's head and pulled the trigger.

* * *

Colonel Garibaldi flinched when he heard the shot and reached up to touch his cross.

James laughed again. "It's not going to be that easy, Spencer Barnett. . . . You are going to suffer a lot before I kill you." He nodded at the guards, and they started pushing the dirt in around Spencer. "Keep your arms down at your sides or I'll have the guards break them."

Spencer sat with his eyes closed and felt the cool earth against his skin. The guards packed the red clay down around his neck, using the butts of their AK-47s.

"You have a good night's sleep. I'll stop by later on, and then, *maybe*, I'll kill you . . . if you beg nice." James strolled back to the longhouse he shared with his Montagnard woman. She was the only Bru who hadn't escaped . . . yet.

Barnett thought only about good things. He had decided that he wasn't going to die bitter, thinking about the pain that wracked his body. He was going to die thinking about good things. He let his mind slip back to South Carolina. The years he had spent in the foster care system had produced only one good set of foster parents, and they had *really* loved him. He had fit right into the family as the younger brother to the only child his foster parents had. They didn't play any favorites and treated him exactly as they did their own son. What was unusual was that their son accepted him as his younger brother. Spencer had loved living on their farm, even the good-night kisses. At first he acted like he didn't like it when they came into his room to say good night. He was eleven years old, and kissing old people, especially his foster father, was for perverts, but when they were late coming to his room and he thought they had forgotten him, he would almost cry. Those were good times, until the social worker decided that he was becoming too close to his foster family and it would be better to transfer him to another home. He still couldn't figure out why they had done that to him. He went berserk and broke the social worker's nose and kicked one of her helpers in the nuts. They declared him emotionally unstable and placed him in a juvenile home that was over ninety-five percent poor southern blacks. He had gone into the juvenile system a normal, happy boy right off a farm with loving, caring people around him and had come out—after being treated by professional psychiatrists, psychologists, and social workers—a hostile, prejudiced, mistrusting teenager. He joined the army to escape from the emotional vampires who were feeding off him.

Spencer changed his thoughts to the Recondo School and Master Sergeant McDonald. He had been attracted to the man in a very strange way. He felt that there was more to the professional soldier than the man would allow people to see. Spencer had been around a lot, especially when he was in the juvenile center, and he had been propositioned by men and women alike. McDonald wasn't like that; he was the kind of person you would want for a father. That was it! Spencer finally figured out what attracted him to the master sergeant—he was the perfect father figure.

Barnett smiled and felt a beetle crawl next to his neck. He tried twisting his chin against the ground, but it only made the insect more determined to burrow next to his neck behind his ear. His body had warmed the dirt that was packed around it, and he was comfortable except for the cramped position he was sitting in. He let his mind slip and remembered what he was sitting on and felt a rush of nausea.

Good thoughts! He had to think good thoughts. Fishing . . . swimming in the cool farm ponds . . . running after the coon hounds. Good thoughts!

"You sleeping, motherfucker?" James had returned in the dark.

Spencer didn't answer.

"I said, are you sleeping!"

Spencer remained quiet.

"Well, I don't give a fuck if you are!" James plopped down less than a foot from Spencer's exposed head and reached out to feel in the dark for his ex-teammate. He touched Spencer's dew-covered head. "You honkies are all alike. Your hair is too fucking soft!" James ran his hand through Spencer's hair like a man would do to his dog. "Why have you been so hard on me, Spence?" James's voice was friendly. The scotch was talking now. "What the fuck did I ever do to you? It's fucking hardass honkies like you who make us like we are."

Spencer tried turning his head away from the stroking hand.

"So you're awake." James pressed the open end of the scotch bottle against Spencer's lips. "Have a drink." He poured and Spencer gagged.

"I could use some water."

"All right! I'll get you some water if you'll talk to me. I'm sick of talking to myself."

"Get me some water."

James left and returned a few minutes later carrying a tin of water and a piece of fried fish. "Here." He poured the water slowly into Spencer's mouth.

The water tasted better than chocolate ice cream with cherry topping. "Thanks."

"Here's some fish. . . ." James held it out in the dark for Spencer to eat. "Why have you been so hard on me? I just wanted to be your friend."

"Why have you turned against your country?"

"I haven't! If those motherfuckers back in Detroit would have treated the black people *fair*, we wouldn't have to do this!"

"Do what?" Spencer had no idea what response the question would bring.

James sat quietly drinking from the bottle for a couple of minutes before speaking. "Do you know I was the youngest Death Angel in Detroit?"

"What's a Death Angel?"

"It's part of the militant Moslem movement . . . that's what the whites call us. . . . A Death Angel is *special*. You have to kill five whites to be a Death Angel, and then you have *respect*!"

Spencer tried turning his head so that he could see James in the moonlight, but the dirt was packed too tightly.

"I am the best!" James held the bottle up and toasted the full moon. "I's killed twenty-three whites . . . so far!" He looked at Spencer. "You going to be twenty-*four*."

"Is that why you came to Vietnam?"

"You got it!" James staggered to his feet. "You have fun out here tonight, 'cause in the morning . . . I'm coming back to blow out your fucking brains!"

"Thanks . . ." Spencer put all the sarcasm he could into the single word.

"Ha!" James pulled out his penis and tried urinating on Spencer's head but was too drunk to see where he was aiming and missed completely. "I'll be back in the morning, Spencer!"

The flight of Hueys flew low-level across the border of Laos. There had been no air strikes or artillery prep fires to alert the NVA that they were coming. A forward air controller was already on station ten miles to the west and had five sorties of F-4s on call and two flights of A-1Es. General Seacourt and selected members of his staff were flying in a specially designed airborne command center. The general had the capability of monitoring numerous radio channels and controlling the operation from the large, converted passenger jet. He had direct communications to the commander of all American forces in Vietnam and a line back to the chief of staff in Washington, D.C. The prisoner snatch operation had the highest interest, and its success would be a major boost to morale in South Vietnam.

Master Sergeant McDonald squatted behind the lead ship's pilot and directed him the last few thousand meters to the village and the Montagnard pasture. It was ironic that an NVA general officer had used the same helipad only days earlier.

The team helicopters touched down in a diamond formation. The door gunners sat behind their machine guns, ready to open fire at any NVA targets. They had been instructed that there would be no random firing until the POWs had been located and brought under American control. Surprise was the key element to a successful POW recovery. Any hesitation on the part of the snatch team would result in the deaths of the prisoners. McDonald had learned that lesson well.

Woods hopped off his chopper before it touched the ground and rolled over one shoulder, then back up on his feet, running toward the buildings before the next man left the aircraft. Sergeant Lee San Ko was right behind him. The rest of the team, in fire teams of two, spread out and assaulted their assigned targets.

Lieutenant Van Pao woke with a start when she heard the helicopters landing. She rolled off her cot, reached for the telephone, and turned the hand crank. The instant she heard a voice answer, she screamed into the handset that her camp was under attack by Americans. The duty sergeant at her division headquarters alerted the infantry company that had been assigned to react in the event that A Rum was assaulted by a rescue party. The NVA company had been hidden in the jungle five hundred meters away from the village, and its prime mission was to support the A Rum camp. Only Lieutenant Van Pao knew that the division commander had taken that precaution.

Mohammed James was still very drunk and lay naked next to his Montagnard slave girl. She heard the helicopters and slipped off the mat to look out of the shuttered window. Escape had always been on her mind, and she was hoping that the steel birds were bringing Americans instead of the hated NVA.

James opened his red-rimmed eyes and tried lifting his head off the rolled mat he used for a pillow. "Ahhh . . . it's fucking morning already. Shit!" He closed his eyes. "Today I blow away Spencer Barnett!"

Colonel Garibaldi had heard the choppers coming for a couple of minutes. He was an Air Force officer and had an ear for the sounds of aircraft. He could tell that they were coming from the east and that there were a lot of them. He lay flat on his mat in case they bombed and prepped the village before landing.

Once on land, the Special Forces recon team found the South Vietnamese POW longhouse. The POWs had been chained to their cots. Lieutenant Nappa and Sergeant Cooper started cutting through the chains with their bolt cutters. One of the South Vietnamese officers spoke English. "Give me the cutters! You *kill* the guards!" Nappa handed the soldier the bolt cutters.

"Are there any Americans here?" Cooper asked over his shoulder as he watched the exit.

"Yes! They're being kept in cages. Over there about fifty feet in the jungle." He pointed.

"Thanks!" Cooper started for the exit.

"Go to the pasture helipad as soon as you can . . . Chinooks will be arriving soon to pick you up!" Nappa pointed back the way they had come. The South Vietnamese officer nodded and barked orders to the prisoners. He left the three Bru tribesmen with the South Vietnamese POWs to protect the group.

Woods was the first one to open fire. He killed five NVA soldiers exiting one of their sleeping hooches. All of the guards had been confused and were waiting for orders. The surprise of the assault had been complete. The NVA guards on duty were killed quickly by the fire teams, except for the two guards with Garibaldi; they had taken up positions next to the colonel's cage, waiting for instructions. They knew that if any Americans appeared, they were to cut the colonel's throat before allowing him to escape.

McDonald and Reed entered the longhouse and saw the Montagnard girl standing spread-legged over James. She was holding a bloody Montagnard ceremonial knife in her hand. The look of extreme hatred on her face did not need to be interpreted.

"Dammit!" McDonald rushed forward and shoved the girl off to one side. He leaned over the soldier and checked for a heartbeat. James was still alive, but bleeding badly from the wound in his chest. "We've got to save him, Lieutenant! This is one man I want to see face a court-martial!"

"Go! I'll give him first aid and carry him back to the choppers!" Lieutenant Reed waved with his CAR-15 toward the door. He knew that McDonald was looking for Barnett.

"Thanks!" The sergeant ran out of the longhouse, holding his weapon at the ready.

Nappa and Cooper broke through the thick jungle into the POW clearing before they could stop. The guards opened fire. Cooper rolled over on his side and instinctively fired a burst. The guards ducked down behind Garibaldi's cage, giving Nappa enough time to assault. There was no time for any kind of delay. Nappa knew that he would die or live, and the next five seconds would decide which one would happen. The guards were not expecting a frontal assault and were caught by surprise. Nappa killed both of them.

Garibaldi looked up from his mat and saw the camouflaged face of the Special Forces officer. "Thank God!"

Nappa saw that the gate to the cage was locked. He shook his head angrily because he had left the bolt cutters behind. He saw that the bamboo bars were tied with bamboo and removed his Randall survival knife from its sheath and began hacking at the bindings. The knife cut through the strands quickly, and he tore apart the bars so Garibaldi could squeeze out between them.

"I thought there was another American." Cooper had been acting as guard.

"There was, but they shot him last night...." Garibaldi felt sick. Spencer had missed being rescued by a single day.

"Where's his body? We'll take it out with us." Nappa turned a full circle with his CAR-15 ready as he spoke.

"Back over there is where I heard the pistol shot. It can't be more than fifty meters away."

"Can you walk?" Nappa looked at the frail man.

"*Today* I can walk as far as you want me to!" Garibaldi felt his heart beating faster. He looked toward Spencer's cage, hoping that they had sneaked him back inside during the night, but it was empty. His eyes rested on Mother Kaa's cage. The huge python was coiled up in one corner. Her skin had dried out and was turning white in large spots. She was a prisoner too. "Let me use your knife, Lieutenant." Garibaldi held out his hand.

"Why?"

"There's another POW that needs to be helped." Garibaldi took the knife and walked over to Mother Kaa's cage.

"Holy shit!" Cooper saw the huge python for the first time. "What the fuck is that!" He couldn't believe his eyes.

Colonel Garibaldi hacked at the knots that held the bamboo poles in place where she lay coiled up. Her weight popped the bindings against the poles she was coiled against when Garibaldi had cut only partially through them. Part of her coils fell out onto the ground, and the colonel stepped back away from her. "You're free, Mother Kaa . . . you're free to go home."

"Come on!" Nappa was getting nervous. "Let's get the other POW's body."

Woods and Lee broke through the edge of the jungle ten meters away from Nappa and Cooper.

"*Shit!*" Cooper blinked. He had nearly fired, thinking they had been NVA, but all of their training had paid off. Every target during a POW snatch had to be *positively* identified before firing. POWs could be running around all over a camp during a snatch.

"Where's Spencer!" Woods screamed the words when he saw only one old man standing with Nappa.

Colonel Garibaldi pointed in the direction he had heard the shot come from the previous night.

Woods took off running in the direction the colonel was pointing. He held his CAR-15 in one hand with his finger on the trigger and the safety off. Woods followed the narrow path through the thick undergrowth and ran fifteen feet out into the clearing before he could bring himself to a stop. He nearly kicked Spencer in the face.

"Oh *God!*" Woods dropped his CAR-15 in the dirt and fell to his knees. "Oh God, what have they done to you,

Spence?" He placed a hand on each of Barnett's cheeks and tried lifting the soldier's head out of the dirt.

Sergeant Lee San Ko stepped out in the clearing seconds after Woods. He saw Woods on his knees in the dirt holding Barnett's head in his hands. It looked to him as if Barnett had been decapitated. He felt like puking and gagged instead. Sergeant Lee saw the NVA soldier step out of the jungle, but she had the advantage and fired first. The AK-47 rounds drove his body back into the jungle.

Barnett opened his eyes at the sound of the automatic weapon and saw Woods's face. "David?" His voice was a whisper.

"He's alive!" Woods screamed the words, ignoring the NVA lieutenant who was swinging her weapon over to where he sat in the dirt.

Barnett's eyes focused, and he saw the CAR-15 rounds from Nappa's weapon tear into the woman's chest. Her back arched and she fell to the ground, dead. Barnett smiled and the blood flowed from his cracked lips, but he didn't care. Sweet Bitch was dead.

"Help me!" Woods screamed and started digging with his hands in the lose soil around Spencer's head. Nappa acted as guard while Woods and Cooper dug with their hands. Colonel Garibaldi tried helping, but his efforts were extremely weak. He had thought he was in pretty good shape, until he saw how fast the healthy Americans were digging. He gave up after a couple of minutes and sat down to rest.

"Take it easy." Lieutenant Nappa handed the colonel Woods's CAR-15, just in case they got some company before they were through digging him out.

Garibaldi took the weapon. "Thanks . . ." He felt useful.

Woods and Cooper dug Barnett out down to his elbows, and then Woods straddled the hole and pulled Spencer out. The odor that followed Spencer out of the hole was extremely foul. "What is that smell?" Woods set Spencer down on the ground next to the open hole and looked back down inside. He could see a small hand sticking out of the dirt and realized that Spencer had been sitting on top of a small child's body. "Those motherfuckers!" A clump of dirt broke loose from the side of the hole and fell down to cover the exposed hand. Only Woods had seen it.

Spencer groaned and drew Woods's attention away from the hole. He was lying on his side but his legs were still curled up under him. Woods tried straightening out his legs and Spencer screamed.

"Just carry him. Once the blood works its way back into his legs, they'll straighten out." Colonel Garibaldi reassured Woods that he hadn't hurt his friend.

"Are there any more POWs?" Nappa asked the colonel.

"There are some South Vietnamese being held back in the longhouses."

"We've already found them."

"And there's James. . . ." Garibaldi's voice lowered.

Barnett heard the names and raised his head off the dirt. *"Kill him . . . David . . . kill him!"*

Nappa looked puzzled. "Where's James?"

"He turned traitor and is working with the NVA." Garibaldi frowned. "He's dangerous, and I agree with Spencer. . . . If you see a black soldier, kill him. He won't be taken alive."

Woods picked up Barnett and carried him in his arms. "Let's get back to the helipad."

The other three Americans joined him, with Cooper taking the lead and Nappa bringing up the rear.

Lieutenant Reed threw James over his shoulder in a fireman's carry and ran back to the waiting Chinook that was loaded with the South Vietnamese POWs. The chopper took off as soon as he hopped on board. Gunships opened fire on the jungle that bordered the open pasture on the sides away from the village. The Chinook took a dozen rounds of 12.7mm antiaircraft fire in its rear section but made a good escape.

McDonald tied in with Arnason and Kirkpatrick and they fought their way through the guards over to Lieutenant Van Pao's office. It was empty. Kirkpatrick threw a white phosphorous grenade into the building, and the hooch burst into flames.

McDonald saw Sergeant Cooper appear around the corner of a longhouse, followed by Woods, who was carrying a small man wearing only the bottom part of a peasant's suit. A taller man followed wearing the same black pajamas, but he carried a CAR-15, and then Lieutenant Nappa shot around the corner, turning around to check their rear. The man in Woods's arms was covered with dirt and filth, but McDonald knew who he was.

"Let's go!" McDonald signaled the men with him, and they started withdrawing to the helipad.

A pair of Huey slicks waited on the pasture with their skids barely touching the ground. The pilots were anxious to load up and get the hell out of there. The landing zone was becoming very hot. Just as McDonald's team arrived at the LZ, a pair of NVA gunners fired their RPG-7s. The twin choppers exploded in balls of flame and collapsed in junk heaps on the green grass that turned black from the heat almost instantly.

"*Go to our alternate LZ!*" McDonald barked the order and waved the team back.

The FAC pilot circling above the LZ saw the helicopters explode and then saw the mass of NVA soldiers approaching the LZ from the jungle. "The LZ is too hot! Abort! Abort!" He screamed over his radio for the remaining rescue choppers to pull away.

The second pair of choppers were already making their approach and could see the Americans standing at the edge of the LZ. The chopper flying in closest to the jungle banked to its left and flew over the top of the other aircraft to escape the ground fire.

The remaining chopper continued its approach on course. The pilot kept his hands on both levers as he made his touchdown. He had been one of the oldest men to have graduated from flight school and had taken a lot of ribbing by the younger trainees because of his age. They had nicknamed him Pappy, and the name had stuck. He was living up to his name; Pappy to everyone, he wasn't going to leave any of his children down there on the ground.

The door gunners had started out firing short bursts from their machine guns, but the NVA targets became so abundant, they ended up just holding down the butterfly triggers on their weapons and moving the barrels from one group of targets to another.

McDonald saw the chopper coming in under the intense ground fire and started spraying the jungle. His team followed suit as they ran for the last extraction aircraft. Nappa, Cooper, and Colonel Garibaldi ran around to the left side of the chopper, and Woods, carrying Barnett, went to the right side with McDonald and the rest of the team.

McDonald, Kirkpatrick, and Arnason were spraying the jungle while the rest of the men loaded up. The engine from the chopper screamed for them to hurry up. Holes popped in the skin of the vehicle everywhere. A round went through the Plexiglas in front of Pappy and nicked his left foot pedal and veered up to smash into his right kneecap. The chopper jerked its tail around to the right, forcing McDonald and the other men outside of the Huey to drop to the ground to escape being cut up by the rear prop. Pappy's hand involuntarily jerked, and the chopper started banking away from the LZ. He tried banking back, but the maneuver was causing him to lose his lift and airspeed, and if he continued banking back to the LZ the chopper would crash. He gave it more power and continued pulling away. He would make a circle and return to pick up the remaining three men.

"Let's go, Pappy!" His copilot screamed over the intercom system.

"We can't!"

"Yes! Look down there!"

Pappy looked down over his left shoulder and saw the LZ covered with brown uniforms. His copilot was right. They couldn't go back. The air was filled with green tracers flying up at them. He banked away from the LZ and headed for the Special Forces camp at A Shau. The chopper left a stream of black smoke behind it as it limped toward the camp.

McDonald saw the black smoke and hoped that they would make it. He slipped back into the jungle with Arnason and Kirkpatrick. The NVA unit was concentrating on the chopper and gave them time to escape. McDonald led the way through the burning POW camp and into the jungle on the opposite side. He passed the cages where the Americans had been held and saw a narrow trail leading off into the jungle. He pointed with his CAR-15, and Arnason took the point, followed by Kirkpatrick.

Mother Kaa was a hundred meters ahead of them. She was using the trail to get down to the river. Arnason nearly stepped on her tail and did a series of quick high-steps to miss her weaving coils. He looked like a football trainee running through tires. Kirkpatrick saw Arnason running funny and then saw the huge python.

"Hot fuck!" The New York soldier had never seen a snake that big.

McDonald caught up to him and slapped Kirkpatrick's rear end with the barrel of his CAR-15. "Go around it!" He took the lead and led Kirkpatrick through the jungle growth around the snake and then back onto the trail. *"Move it!"* Arnason was out of sight and Kirkpatrick ran hard to catch up to him.

Mother Kaa was pissed. She was sick of those smelly things bothering her. She slipped off the trail, and the cool, damp vegetation felt good against her dry skin. She would be very happy if she never saw another one of those creatures again in her life. She flicked out her tongue and sensed the air. The taste and smell of water made her feel at home as she neared the river.

CHAPTER NINE

Gray Justice

The Bru chief pointed in the direction of A Rum, and his men separated into teams of four and disappeared into the jungle. Some of the Bru warriors were armed only with their long knives and crossbows, and a few of them carried NVA AK-47s and SKS semiautomatic rifles. The old chief had served as a scout for the French and knew how modern weapons worked, and fourteen of his villagers had served at one time or another with the Special Forces CIDG program. He had one hundred and seven warriors with him and another fifty Bru men loyal to him at A Shau. The torture and death of his grandson would be avenged.

McDonald let Arnason break trail until the sound of gunfire from the village became muffled, then he signaled for the small, three-man team to stop. Kirkpatrick took up a prone position on the trail facing the direction they had come from. He had the safety off his CAR-15. Arnason took up the same position but faced down the trail in the direction of the Rao Lao River.

McDonald squatted between the two men's feet and spoke in a low whisper. "Turn on your transponders." He reached up on his own web gear and pushed the switch that would send out a signal to Brigadier General Seacourt's airborne command aircraft. "If we get separated, head due east until you reach the valley. At Ta Bat, the Rao Lao turns due south. Stay with the river until you reach the Special Forces camp. Remember that we're on the north side of the Rao Lao, so you'll have to cross over it. I recommend you do that as soon as you can, because it gets wider and deeper in the valley."

Kirkpatrick and Arnason kept their eyes on the trail while McDonald talked. "I'm going to try and avoid all contact with the NVA. . . . There are too many of them for us, and even though we might kill a few of them, they'll eventually surround us by zeroing in on the sound of our weapons." McDonald tapped Arnason's boot. "I'll take point."

The river appeared sooner than McDonald had expected. Moving downhill was easy, and they were making very good time. He picked up an animal trail and headed east next to the swift-running water.

The NVA squad left the cages where the Americans had been kept and started running at a fast clip down the trail. The NVA point man could see the distinctive boot prints in the moist dirt that identified the Americans. They knew that three of them had run back into the village after the helicopter left the LZ. The NVA point man ran with a smile on his face. The Americans were heading down to the Rao Lao, and he was sure that they would turn east and try to make it back to the American base in the A Shau. Americans were fools, they were so predictable.

The Montagnard team watched the three Americans pass through their ambush site. Any one of the small brown men could have reached out and touched the Americans, but their camouflage was perfect. The leader of the team thought that one of the Americans looked like the young soldier who had buried his son and wondered if American fathers loved their children as much as the Bru did.

The NVA squad had made up the distance quickly between them and the three Americans. They ran without worrying about running into an enemy patrol. The first four NVA crashed into the brush lining the trail and rolled downhill until they had become so entangled in vines and bamboo that their bodies stopped. The squad leader had little time to realize what was happening; there were no warning gunshots. The Bru reloaded their crossbows with practiced skill and speed, and three more of the NVA fell down on the trail with small arrows embedded in their throats. The remaining NVA soldier started backing up and bumped into his squad leader. The soldier cursed and tried shoving the man away from him, using his pistol. The blow from the long knife was so swift that the NVA squad leader probably could have looked back and seen his own headless body as his decapitated head spun down on the trail. Only the remaining NVA soldier had time to pull the trigger on his AK-47.

McDonald stopped and turned around to face back down the trail, his CAR-15 held up against his inner thigh. The AK firing had come from less than a hundred meters away. He quickly pointed for Arnason and Kirkpatrick to take up ambush positions next to the trail.

The Bru father used his long ceremonial machete to trim nine two-inch-thick bamboo stakes from the stands of bamboo growing wild next to the trail. The Bru warriors worked fast, impaling the NVA soldiers on the stakes in the same fashion that had been used on his son. Those NVA soldiers were lucky: they were already dead. But the Bru were sending a signal to the living NVA. It took two of the Bru warriors to free the body of the last NVA from the vines he had rolled up in as he had slid down the steep incline. The father waited on the trail with his cousin. The NVA soldier the warriors dragged back had been hit in the lung by the arrow and was still breathing deeply, trying to stay alive; the Bru father nodded and they lifted him and shoved him down on the stake.

McDonald heard the horrible man scream and shivered. Something was happening up the trail. No NVA had passed their ambush. McDonald decided that he would risk leaving the ambush site; they couldn't afford to waste time hiding next to the trail. He left his hiding place slowly and started walking east on the narrow trail. Kirkpatrick constantly kept his eyes on their six o'clock and walked sideways and backward as the small team moved away from the screams.

She had heard the loud noises coming from the plateau and raised her head off her paws. She was very hungry, and it had been days since she had heard that pleasant sound. There would be good things to eat when the loud noises stopped. She got up on her feet and stretched. A soft mewing brought her around, and she licked both of her cubs. They had not had the benefit of a full fifteen weeks inside of their mother but had been born early. The female cub was very weak and would probably die. The small male cub struggled to find his mother's warm body in the large cave. She purred to comfort them and left the entrance of her cave. She must find food so that she could produce the milk her cubs demanded.

McDonald was still serving as the point man when they ran into her on the trail. She was as surprised as they were. The sounds that were loud and shook the ground always left dead things, and here in front of her were live things. The second of confusion gave McDonald the advantage, and he pulled the trigger on his CAR-15. She roared and leaned back on her haunches. Something was stinging her. She turned her head to one side and swatted at the air. McDonald's clip emptied fast. Arnason stepped up next to him and emptied his CAR-15 into the huge tigress. Blood spurted out of her mouth and turned her teeth red. She growled again, but with less force; something was happening that she did not understand. She couldn't move or even swat with her paws.

She died.

"Look at the size of that thing!" Arnason instantly recalled Fillmore being dragged out of his night rest site and wondered if this beast was the one that had eaten him. He didn't know exactly where they were, but they had to be within ten miles of where it had happened.

"Man! This is some shit! First a fucking snake as long as a

fucking *train,* and now a fucking tiger that looks like a motherfucking elephant!" Kirkpatrick shook his head. "Man! This is some *shit!*"

McDonald tended to agree with the New York soldier. The tigress was huge and would have been a world-class trophy except for the scarred, burned hide on her hip. "Move it!" McDonald kept the point and changed magazines as they traveled. The pause from the encounter with the tigress brought McDonald's attention to the dimming light. It would be dark within an hour. He couldn't believe that the day had passed so quickly! They had attacked the POW camp at first light of morning. He couldn't believe his eyes, and waited until they broke out of the jungle to see if it was just thick cloud-cover over the sun or if it had gotten dark. The trail turned to his left and started going up a steep incline. McDonald stayed with it. Animal trails were always the easiest avenues to travel in the jungle. The paths always followed the best terrain.

A half-hour later they broke out of the jungle into a large, rock-covered clearing. McDonald saw that a number of large caves dominated the cliffs above them and a steep drop-off went down to the white-water river. McDonald signaled a break and searched the area for signs of any enemy activity. The sky had turned dark, but not due to normal nightfall; a huge rain cloud was moving in over the whole mountain and valley floor. A raindrop that looked like a gallon of water hit the boulder McDonald was leaning against, followed by another one at his feet. A summer storm was about to break loose, and McDonald knew that trying to walk a mountain trail during one of the heavy downpours would be nearly impossible. Flash floods would roar down the narrow ravines, and the mountainsides would become slides of mud. As he searched the area for shelter, his eyes came to rest on the mouth of a cave.

"Up there!" McDonald pointed with his CAR-15.

Arnason took the lead and climbed slowly up the rocks. Where there was one tiger, there could be two. His thoughts went to the breeding habits of the big cats. Did they mate for life? He wished he had paid attention during his high school biology classes.

The cave didn't go back as far into the mountain as the large entranceway suggested. It did go back enough to protect the three men from the storm that broke out in a fury the instant Kirkpatrick had stepped under its lip.

"It's dry." McDonald remained squatting with his CAR-15 ready as he looked in the back of the cave.

"Smells like an animal lives here." Arnason sniffed the air. "Maybe the tiger's cave?"

"Could be . . ." McDonald turned slowly and swept the cave with his weapon.

"I ain't staying here!" Kirkpatrick stepped toward the entrance.

"I think we killed the occupant. . . . Tigers don't stay together unless they're mating or it's a mother with cubs. . . ." McDonald spoke while his eyes continued searching the cave. The roar from the storm almost drowned out his voice. "In either case, we would have seen the other tigers by now. . . . It's safe."

"How do you know this was *that* tiger's cave?" Kirkpatrick still wasn't too happy with the idea of staying in a tiger's cave.

"They can't stand to live close together. . . . This cave is too close to where we killed it." McDonald hoped he remembered correctly about what he had learned from the *National Geographic* special he had seen on tigers.

"It doesn't matter . . . we can't go out there now." Arnason nodded to the solid sheet of water falling in front of the cave entrance.

The three soldiers took up positions around the cave that gave them as much coverage of the entrance as they could get. The temperature dropped sharply with the rain, and McDonald felt himself shivering in the dampness. For the first time that day he had time to reflect on the events. Barnett was safe. He was sure the chopper made it back safely with him on it. He would have liked to have found James, but getting Barnett back was the important thing. He tried remembering how many men he had lost, but couldn't come up with a number because of the fast action. When they got back to the A-camp, he would find out. They did catch the NVA totally off guard. He wondered where the NVA group that had attacked the helipad had come from. There was no intelligence on a reserve force near the POW camp. McDonald inhaled a deep breath and sighed. With luck, they would be at the camp in the morning. He wouldn't risk traveling at night.

A soft mewing came from the back of the cave.

"Shit!" Kirkpatrick flipped the safety off his weapon. "What the fuck was that?"

"Relax, Kirkpatrick . . . I'll check." Arnason struggled to his feet and walked slowly to the back of the cave. He stopped and flipped his CAR-15 over his shoulder and let it hang from its strap.

"What did you find?" McDonald kept his weapon at the ready.

Arnason reached down and turned around holding a tiny tiger cub in each hand by the scruff of its neck.

"She was a mother. . . ." McDonald lowered his weapon.

"How do you know it was a *she*?" Kirkpatrick still wasn't happy.

"I checked." McDonald smiled and relaxed. He was sure now that the cave had belonged to the large female tiger they had killed on the trail. "Bring them over here." He held out his hands, and Arnason gave him the smallest one. "They're premature." He turned her around and looked at the scrawny cub. "You would never believe how big their mother was by looking at them."

"What should we do with them?" Arnason still held the cub by its neck skin.

McDonald shrugged his shoulders. "Let's take them with us." He opened the front of his jacket and stuffed the cub inside. She wiggled and hissed until she felt the warmth, and then she settled down and began purring. Arnason stuffed his cub into his shirt and the same thing occurred. "They're going to get a little hungry until we get back, but they should make it."

"Man! I don't think fucking around with tiger cubs is a good idea!" Kirkpatrick still wasn't sold on the idea.

"What should we do? Kill them?" McDonald felt bad about killing their mother, even though he knew she would have killed them without a second thought.

"Fuck it!" Kirkpatrick went back to the entrance of the cave and looked out. "It's beginning to stop. . . ."

McDonald stepped out of the cave. The rain had stopped, but wide rivers of runoff were cascading down the slope, which made walking dangerous. He knew that staying in the cave much longer would also bring danger. The NVA would have to be close behind them. He decided on risking the trail.

The Montagnards left the shelter of the large tree and got back on the trail. The dead tigress lying next to the trail explained the automatic weapons they had heard firing earlier, just before the rain. The Montagnard boy's father stopped his team and ordered them to skin the dead beast. She was too great a prize to let rot. He lifted one of her paws and released a lungful of air in awe. The tiger's paw was bigger than both of his hands held side by side. She was huge. He forced the claws to extend from her paw and smiled. A necklace would be made from her claws that would become legendary among all of the tribes. It was a good sign that Ae Die had returned to the Bru and that the evil one, Tang Lie, was gone with the fire that had destroyed their village and the NVA. The Bru worked quickly on the tigress and hid the skin in the hollow branch of a dying mahogany tree.

Brigadier General Seacourt was monitoring McDonald's movement on the ground almost by the meter. He had ordered the Special Forces camp to send out company-sized patrols to link up with the small American team as soon as they crossed over the border. The general told the camp commander over the secure voice radio that he hoped he wasn't too good at map reading. The Green Beret teams had been positioned near the border under secret orders a couple of days before the mission.

McDonald stopped when they reached a small mountain stream that had turned into a ten-foot-wide rapids. He looked for a way to cross the fast-moving water and couldn't find one.

"We could jump. . . ." Kirkpatrick had been a broad jumper in high school, and the ten feet would be easy for him.

"Not with all our gear and weapons. The other side is muddy." McDonald pointed with the barrel of his CAR-15.

"I can do it and you can bring my stuff across. The water is only a couple feet deep." Kirkpatrick removed his web gear and handed it to Arnason. He gave his weapon to McDonald. "Cut a couple long bamboo poles and hand them across to me once I'm over there. You can wade across and I'll pull you with the pole. . . ."

"Good idea, Kirk . . ." It was the first time Arnason had used a nickname for Kirkpatrick. The New Yorker had changed since his buddy's death and was a super soldier.

Kirkpatrick made the jump with ease—he probably could have made it with his gear on. McDonald held the pole out, and Kirkpatrick grabbed hold of it and stuffed four feet of the bamboo under his arm. McDonald entered the fast-moving water and almost lost his footing on the slippery bottom. The force against his legs was tremendous. He couldn't lift either foot without being swept away. "Pull!"

Kirkpatrick saw the predicament McDonald was in and started pulling him along the bottom of the flash-flood stream by pulling the pole toward him, hand over hand. Once McDonald had cleared land, he laid his gear down and helped Kirkpatrick repeat the process with Arnason.

The American team then followed the contour lines of the hills and headed due east. They weren't going to waste any time by trying to throw off any pursuers. The jungle was thinning out and the team could see F-4 jets and gunships making passes toward the village of A Rum and the NVA defenders.

The voice came out of the jungle: "We're friends . . . Sergeant McDonald!" There were no bodies to be seen in the wall of vegetation.

McDonald dropped down in a combat crouch.

The voice repeated itself: "We're friends . . . from A Shau . . . Special Forces. . . ."

"Show yourselves, slowly." McDonald moved the barrel of his weapon toward the spot in the jungle the voice had come from.

One of the plants moved and a perfectly camouflaged Green Beret stepped out of the jungle onto the narrow trail. Arnason was amazed because as alert as he had been, his small team would have passed within five feet of the camouflaged Special Forces sergeant and his Bru commando team and not have detected them.

"Let's go! I'll guide you back to the LZ. The general is waiting for you back at the CCN compound."

One of the tiger cubs mewed.

"What's that?" The SF sergeant started to drop down. He was totally alert for anything to happen.

"Tiger cub." McDonald unbuttoned the front of his shirt and the cub stuck its head out and called for its mother. She was hungry. So was McDonald.

The Green Beret sergeant raised his eyebrows but said nothing, and gave a hand signal for the team to slip back into the neutral jungle.

Epilogue

The whole atmosphere at the Command and Control North compound was jubilant. The success of the prisoner snatch mission spread like wildfire over the Special Forces radio network. The Marine Corps guards located atop Marble Mountain fired multicolored hand flares when the helicopter carrying McDonald, Arnason, and Kirkpatrick arrived at the CCN pad.

Brigadier General Seacourt was waiting for the chopper to land, along with half of the Green Berets in the camp. Even though only two Americans had been rescued, the event was a landmark mission. Five of the South Vietnamese in the POW camp were commandos from CCN, and the success of the mission proved that the North Vietnamese system of rotating POWs from camp to camp had failed and that Americans were capable of rescuing their own people. The ill-fated Song Tay raid in the north had totally demoralized the troops; nothing had been spared in support of the operation, and yet it had fallen flat on its face. So the A Rum raid was a sweet victory.

McDonald was the first one off the chopper. He smiled shyly when the men started clapping and whistling. Kirkpatrick took a New York bow and then raised his fist above his

178

head in a victory salute. Arnason tried slipping into the crowd.

Seacourt shook hands with McDonald. He didn't even try talking above the noise and waved the three-man team over to his jeep. The top had been removed, and the team jumped in the back with the general riding shotgun. The tiger cub in Arnason's shirt mewed and scratched his stomach when he tried squatting down on the jump seat. Arnason, who had forgotten all about the cub, opened his jacket and removed the young beast, which snarled and spat. The assembled crowd went wild when Arnason held the striped tiger cub up in the air so they all could see it. Seacourt shook his head and smiled. He leaned over and yelled in McDonald's ear, "Where the hell did you find that?"

McDonald opened his jacket and removed the female cub. "The Recondo School has a new mascot, compliments of the NVA!"

Seacourt had his driver take the team directly to the U.S. Navy hospital where the POWs had been taken. He knew without being asked that McDonald would want to see Barnett.

James lay on the clean hospital sheets and watched the black MP sitting in the chair at the foot of his bed. The knife wound the Montagnard girl had inflicted on him was deep, but it had missed his vital organs. He would heal quickly.

"Hey, brother . . . how about unlocking this handcuff and let me stretch."

The MP ignored the wounded soldier.

"Hey, bro!" Mohammed James tried sitting up in the bed. "How about lighting me up a cigarette?"

The black MP continued ignoring James.

"Hey! Motherfucker! Can't you talk?" James screamed out the words.

The MP left his seat and went over to the side of the bed where James's arm was handcuffed to the steel frame. He looked at the smiling soldier and without warning slapped his face. "You shut the fuck up . . . hear?"

"Man! Why did you do that?" James rubbed his stinging cheek. "Us black brothers have got to stick together!"

"Listen good! 'Cause I'm only going to say this *one* time!" The black MP poked his finger against James's bandaged chest. "The *only* reason I don't blow your black ass away is because every decent black soldier in Vietnam is waiting to see your ass *shot* in front of a firing squad!" The look on the MP's face scared James. The MP started turning away from the traitor. "You've set our people back a hundred years! Maybe you don't know it yet, but your picture has been posted in every MP station, PX, company orderly room, and bar in Vietnam!" The MP removed his .45-caliber pistol and cocked the hammer as he pointed it between James's eyes. "So don't you say another damn word to me about being *brothers*."

Seacourt walked next to McDonald as they followed the doctor down the hallway to the room where Barnett and Colonel Garibaldi were being treated.

"I talked with both of them yesterday for a little while. . . ." Seacourt reached over and grabbed McDonald's elbow to slow him down so that he could brief him before they entered the room. "I want you to know that Colonel Garibaldi—he's the other POW with Barnett—has recommended Barnett for the Medal of Honor. . . ." Seacourt paused to let the impact of what he said sink in. "And from just the few things Garibaldi has told me, there won't be a problem. I'm personally going to sign and hand-carry the paperwork to the MACV commanding general and then take it to the Pentagon. If there is one person who has performed above and beyond the call of duty, it's that *teenager* in there!"

McDonald felt tears of extreme pride well up in his eyes. He stopped outside the door and rubbed away the tears; the last thing he needed was to have Barnett see him crying like some pussy-assed baby.

A smile popped on Barnett's face the instant he saw

McDonald step through the door. "Hello, Sergeant McDonald!"

Spencer lay naked on the hospital bed, with only a sheet pulled up to his waist. McDonald could see the red welts covering the soldier's body and the thin ribs showing under his skin. Barnett was emaciated. Jungle ulcers covered half of his chest and right arm.

McDonald swallowed hard. At least the boy was still alive, but from the way he looked, he wouldn't have lasted another week in that camp.

"Can't you talk?" Barnett frowned.

Colonel Garibaldi lay with an IV in his arm, smiling at the three members of his rescue team. He nodded his head and weakly whispered, "Thanks . . ."

McDonald's eyes left Barnett and went to the colonel. He nodded his head, afraid to risk saying anything. There was too much emotion ready to break loose inside of him.

"Sarge! Can't you talk?" Barnett smiled.

McDonald took two quick steps and closed the distance between them. He reached over and hugged Barnett. "I couldn't lose you, kid."

Barnett's smile turned into a wide grin. "Look at this shit! This is disgusting! A *master sergeant* in the United States Army, hugging me!" Barnett loved it.

The other occupants in the room felt lumps creeping up in their throats. General Seacourt coughed and tried breaking the emotional tension. "You could get court-martialed for that, Sergeant!"

Everyone started laughing and the tension broke. The tiger cub was being squashed and growled her anger.

"What was that?" Barnett looked down at McDonald's jacket and saw the movement.

"A friend." He removed the cub and set her down on Barnett's sheet. She moved her head weakly from side to side. One of the nurses who had been watching stepped forward and picked the cub up to check her eyes.

"She's a preemie. . . ."

"Yes . . . and so is her brother." Arnason removed the male.

"Two!" A nurse who had just entered the room shook her head. "We've got an incubator in the back . . ."—she looked over at the hospital commander, who was standing next to General Seacourt, and the doctor nodded his approval— "that we can use. That is, if you want me to try and save them."

Barnett looked hard at the nurse. "Don't I know you from somewhere?"

"No . . . I don't think we've ever met. . . . My name is Natasha MacReal."

"Oh . . . I thought we had met. . . . You're a good-looking woman. . . ." Barnett smiled.

"Well, I can see he's getting better already!" The doctor frowned and waved a finger at the young soldier as the nurse left the room carrying a wiggling tiger cub under each arm.

Barnett turned his attention back to his teammates. "What are you going to name them?"

Arnason shook his head slowly and then spoke. "How about . . . Barnett? We're going to build a cage in front of the recon company's orderly room for him."

"Cool!" Barnett liked the idea. "What about the female?" He looked at McDonald.

"I've already decided on a real good name . . . Spencer."

"*Spencer!*" Barnett feigned outrage and raised himself on one elbow. "Sarge! You ain't going to name no damn *female* Spencer!"

McDonald looked back at the men in the room. "It has a good ring to it . . . Spencer . . . doesn't it?"

The occupants all nodded their heads in agreement.

"Then Spencer it is!"

"Come on, Sarge! Give me a break!"

Arnason laid his hand on McDonald's shoulder. "You know, that *does* have a good sound to it. If the cubs are ever visiting each other, you can say, '*Spencer Barnett!*' and they'll both come to you."

"I really can't believe all of this shit!" Barnett loved all the attention he was getting. He dropped his head back down on the pillow and looked up at the ceiling. The tears bubbled up out of his eyes. "I can't believe this shit. . . ." The emotional dam broke.

The doctor nodded his head toward the door, letting the visitors know that it was time for them to leave.

"Spencer. . ." Brigadier General Seacourt removed the CAR-15 submachine gun he had been carrying over his shoulder. The familiar weapon hadn't drawn any attention until then. "Lieutenant Reed asked me if I would drop this off with you. . . . He said that it was yours." The general had no idea what the weapon meant to Barnett. "He said that you might want it back."

Barnett blinked his eyes and saw his weapon in the general's hand. "Tell . . . tell the lieutenant . . . thanks a lot." He had barely spoken the last word when his throat refused to allow any more words to pass. He buried his face in his pillow and sobbed quietly.

Colonel Garibaldi rubbed the small bamboo cross that he had brought with him out of A Rum and watched the soldiers leave. He had never lost faith.

They were free.

Dear Mom and Dad,

Sorry I haven't written for so long, but when the Army decides to make you busy, there's not much time for anything else.

It's a real sense of accomplishment when a group of guys can pull together and make something really work. (Sorry I can't go into details, but you know how things are with military security and all.) It gives you a sense of pride like you really matter.

Thanks for the cookies. I shared them with Spencer Barnett. I'm real glad he's back with our outfit again.

Love,

David

the trigger and moved his hand a couple of inches to the left of Barrett's head and pulled the trigger.